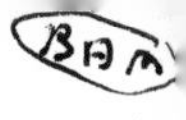

S0-BAR-923

A MARRIAGE WORTH WAITING FOR

A MARRIAGE WORTH WAITING FOR

BY

SUSAN FOX

MILLS & BOON®

First published in Great Britain 2004
Large Print edition 2004
Harlequin Mills & Boon Limited,
Eton House, 18-24 Paradise Road,
Richmond, Surrey TW9 1SR

ISBN 0 263 18104 9

Set in Times Roman 18 on 20 pt.
16-0904-40794

Printed and bound in Great Britain
by Antony Rowe Ltd, Chippenham, Wiltshire

CHAPTER ONE

SELENA KEITH had never been seriously injured before the wreck. She'd been waiting to make a left turn at an intersection when another car had run a red light and hit the driver's side of her car just behind the door. Though she hadn't broken any bones, her body had been soundly pummeled, as had her head. It felt at least six sizes too large, and the pain in it could go from dull to blinding in a punishing flash if she moved too suddenly or exerted herself at all.

She'd been in the hospital since late afternoon the day before. Little more than a half hour ago that morning she'd managed, with help, to get out of bed and sit in a chair for twenty whole minutes.

The difficulty she'd had doing that small thing was as frightening for Selena as it seemed pitiful.

Where had her strength gone? Always vital and physically active, she was stunned at the helplessness she felt now. The stark realization of her own mortality had already laid her spirits as low as her battered body, but this weakness was truly alarming.

Her surprising depression over it mixed toxically with the homesickness she'd kept at bay for two years, and it took most of her puny strength to keep both in check. An ocean of tears churned like bile in her chest, threatening to drown her, but as she'd discovered, giving in to them drained what little energy she had and sent her body and head into such spasms of agony that she'd resolved not to cry.

If she'd sustained something more serious than a concussion, she might be able to accept a hospital stay with a bit more patience, but lying around so much over a knock on the head and a spectacular collection of bruises made her feel like a malingerer.

Selena's eyelids dropped heavily shut barely a moment before she heard the door to her private hospital room open. She'd already grown accustomed to the relentless intrusion of nurses and medical staff, and since it was early yet for visitors, she didn't bother to open her eyes. Perhaps one of the two nurses who'd just settled her back in bed after her little adventure had returned for something, but she was too exhausted to care.

It was the sound of boot heels on tile instead of the smart *swick-swick* of nurse's shoes that alerted her. And then her heart registered the silent thunder of the one presence she'd never forget if she lived to be a hundred.

The approaching boot steps halted at her bedside. The subtle scents of leather and sunshine and the remembered hint of musky aftershave reached for her and sent a wave of longing and dread through her heart. The ocean of tears swelled higher to send a few stinging drops upward in a geyser that made her eyes burn.

"You look like hell."

The gruff words were as gravelly as they were blunt. Morgan Conroe wasn't the sort of man who used soft platitudes or made tactful observations, at least not with her.

That's why she'd left Conroe Ranch. The fact that Morgan had never made a single effort to contact her since the day she'd driven away confirmed she'd made the right decision.

He'd never change his mind about her and she'd never been able to change what she'd stupidly felt for him, so the only sane thing to do had been to clear out. She rallied to protect herself.

"No one asked you to look," she said, then forced her heavy eyelids to open. She knew she looked as weak and pitiful as she felt, so she needed to give some sign of strength to ward him off. "If you came to gloat, go ahead. Take a few jabs then go away."

She made herself get the bold words out before she let herself focus on him, and she was instantly glad she had because the sight of him gave her a disheartening jolt. If she hadn't already been weak, seeing him again would have made her weak. For women like her, men like this one defined the very essence of masculinity.

Hard-bitten and rugged, Morgan Conroe was the quintessential Westerner, a purebred Texan from the crown of his outlaw black Stetson to the bottoms of his underslung heels. Tough, masculine and arrogant, Morg was the kind of man who'd bleed Texas dirt or Lone Star crude if scratched. Part protector and defender of the weak, part vigilante, as autocratic as an old time cattle king, and far too volatile to trifle with or cross. And so overwhelmingly male that he was at least half Neanderthal, though far less predictable and safe.

His weathered face was so permanently tanned that it hinted at a Spanish ancestry, and his expression was, as usual, set in harsh lines. His high cheekbones and black hair emphasized those hints of ancestry, but his eyes were a deep, dark blue that could either frost the soul, or glow like blue flame. Rarely, oh so very rarely, did they go soft with tenderness or sparkle with amusement. It was far more common to see them glitter with irritation or displeasure. Or only a bit less often, to show a blue lightning flash of temper.

He had a certain gruff charm when he wanted to charm, but that was a rare thing, easily overlooked or forgotten since his no-nonsense, my-way-or-the-highway disposition was so prominent. It wasn't in Morgan Conroe's nature to be passive or ambivalent, or to bow or bend to anything or anyone less than his Maker. How she'd survived living under the same roof with him that last five years after she'd fallen so out of favor might qualify as the eighth wonder of the world.

His low, gravelly drawl sent a bracing chill through her heart. "I came to take you home."

It took her a dizzy moment to register the shocking words. The hurt and frustration of both the present and the past reared up, and the pain in her head bloomed so quickly that she reflexively jerked up a hand to make it stop.

"Go away," she whispered, and pressed a palm to her forehead as if to contain the explosion.

The big fingers that closed around her wrist as her weak arm gave out were hot and hard with thick calluses. Morgan lowered her arm to the bed and those hard fingers shifted to warmly clasp her hand. But then his other hand brushed lightly over the top of her head.

"Hurts, don't it, baby." The calm, growling statement sent a warm breath of comfort through her. "Just relax," he said then murmured, almost to himself, "These damned concussions..."

The way he'd said it gave the impression that he was on her side, fighting the injury with her. Which put her heart in peril, though the hurt in her head distracted her from the full impact of that wary observation.

Remarkably, the harsh pain began to subside, and then that big, hard palm began to move in gentle, soothing strokes that avoided the tender place on her skull and reduced the knife blades of pain to a much less awful ache.

Memories of watching Morg with an injured or frightened animal ghosted through her thoughts. There was no one better with animals than Morgan, especially the little ones. For all his brusqueness with people, he had a certain magic with animals and children. The smaller and more helpless or hurt they were, the more they instinctively trusted him.

That was one of the many reasons she'd loved him once upon a time. At twelve, she'd idolized him. She'd been a skinny city kid whose flighty, neglectful mother had married his father. She'd been painfully shy and terrified of horses and cattle and the frightening roughness of ranch life.

But the much older Morg had been kind to her, and so patient that she'd followed him around and hung on his every word. He'd taught her the manly arts of riding, roping, fly-fishing and target shooting, but he'd also instructed her on how well-brought-up young ladies were expected to behave in public.

He'd passed judgment on the length of her hems, had private "man talks" with the boys who'd dared to take her on dates, and he'd taught her to dance. He'd taught her everything she'd needed to know, and he'd made sure she'd had a secure place in his family and in his world.

But all that changed a handful of years later when she'd developed a crush on him. As if he'd sensed it, he'd begun a subtle withdrawal. She no longer got to go everywhere with him. And then he hardly ever let her be around him in situations when they'd be alone.

Hurt by his remoteness, and those first inklings of rejection, Selena had tried all the more to be with him and take part in everything he did. Until that awful, awful time when she'd been seventeen, and frustration, youthful stupidity, and the excruciating pain of unrequited adolescent love had driven her to corner him and confess.

Even now, she couldn't bear to let that memory come. But turning her mind away from it put her attention right back on the soothing movement of his hand.

And the wild, sweet stirrings of the soul-deep feelings for Morgan Conroe that had matured years past adolescence and promised to be even more dangerous to her heart than ever.

Selena found the strength to pull her hand from his and weakly move her head. "S-stop. Please."

Oh God, that had sounded just as forlorn as she felt. But it was torture to have him touch her like this—to touch her at all—when she knew there'd inevitably come a time when he'd again withdraw from her. And then if he somehow sensed how besotted she was—and in spite of everything, she was *still* besotted—he'd reject her as brutally as before.

"All right, little one."

The low rasp went through her hurting body like a warm balm, and she felt the hypnotic pull on her heart. His big hand shifted away from her head, but the back of a knuckle trailed lightly down her cheek. Selena was too weak now to control the flutter of her closed lashes as the pleasure of that registered.

"Get some sleep. Everything's taken care of."

The gruff words sent a quake of happiness and relief through her groggy mind.

Everything's taken care of translated to *I'll take care of you.* Words she might have died to hear from him again, words that common sense warned her to immediately protest, but words too formidable to either reject or ignore in her feeble physical state.

Mercifully, the blackness dropped over her then and dragged her to a place where Morgan Conroe couldn't follow.

"Mr. Conroe made arrangements for you to recover at your family's home. I understand you'll have someone nearby around-the-clock."

The doctor's statement rocked her, but before Selena could protest, his added words kept her silent.

"Otherwise, I couldn't release you for at least another day."

One of the cardinal rules she'd lived by all her life—to keep family dirt private—ensured her silence now. Growing up, she'd never mentioned family problems to outsiders because she'd been ashamed of her mother's behavior and their gypsy life. Then after her mother had married Morgan's father, she'd kept silent about her mother's secrets, the fibs, the infidelities, the little manipulations.

She'd suffered her crush for her stepbrother without telling anyone, not even her mother, until she'd made the colossal mistake of telling Morgan himself. And of course, keeping to habit, she'd never told a soul about his angry rejection either.

So Selena felt even less inclined to inform the doctor that she had no "family" home. There was no reason for him to know that the only home she counted these days—or wanted—was her apartment.

The goal now was to get out of this depressing place. Once the doctor authorized her release, she'd call a cab and make a quick escape before Morgan came around again. He'd only been here that one time yesterday morning, so if she was lucky, she could be gone before he showed up again.

Obviously Morg had talked to the doctor about her release, but she hoped he'd done that over the phone. She'd had a friend bring her a set of clothes last night, though Selena hadn't known for sure that she'd have a chance of being released today.

That morning she'd awakened with a bit more energy, so she felt more eager than ever to leave the hospital. Her IV had been removed, her take-home med would be ready soon, so the moment the doctor strode out, she called a cab company and gingerly slipped out of bed.

As she quickly discovered, it was a challenge to dress. The stiff pain that plagued her every move left her sitting weakly in the chair, her head spinning and her skin lightly sheened with perspiration.

If she could get to her apartment, she'd be fine. She'd be able to lie down and sleep uninterrupted. A day or so of quality rest and her body would surely begin to make real progress toward recovery. Just being home was bound lift her dismal spirits.

A nurse came in with a clipboard of papers for her to sign, and the flowers and plants that friends had brought or sent were loaded onto a cart while an aide gathered up a bag of her things, including her clothes from the wreck and the take-home painkiller.

In the midst of the efficient activity a wheelchair was brought into the room, and Selena gratefully moved to it from the chair. The tiny parade of cart and wheelchair rolled rapidly through the maze of corridors and elevators to arrive on the sidewalk outside the outpatient door.

She'd made it. There was no sign of Morgan and neither the nurse nor the aide commented on the taxi, so perhaps they'd either not been informed of the doctor's requirements for her release or they'd assumed the taxi would take her to the "family" home.

Selena was certain she could manage on her own, whatever the doctor thought, as long as she didn't have to go out for anything. Friends had already volunteered to come by and give her a hand or pick up a few groceries when she needed them. All she had to do was get home.

Just then a dark green Suburban pulled into the pick up zone and glided to a halt behind the taxi. Selena didn't need to see the Conroe Ranch logo on the side to know Morgan had arrived to thwart her plan.

He left the engine running and got out, taking a moment to walk briskly to the cab driver. A quick word and a handshake, which she knew would discretely pass the driver a large denomination bill for his trouble, effectively closed her single avenue of escape. And then Morg was striding around the back of the taxi to where she and her things were parked by the curb.

Morgan's low, "Hey there, Selly," and the faint smile that softened the harsh line of his mouth implied friendship and closeness, and Selena's gaze shot away from his. The sweet nostalgia of hearing him call her by the old nickname caught her by surprise and brought back a wealth of good times best forgotten that contrasted sharply with her anger at him now.

The weariness that gripped her only stoked her outrage at his high-handedness and her failure to thwart it. Both the nostalgic feelings and her anger combined to create a churn of upset that drained her even more. Her head was pounding again, and all she wanted to do was crawl into a cave somewhere to escape both the pain and all things Conroe.

As Morgan directed the nurse and the aide to wheel her and the cart to his SUV, Selena felt her frustration rush higher. She couldn't imagine what all this was about. For more than two years, she'd heard nothing directly from Morg, though she knew he had her address because she received profit checks from her small share of Conroe Ranch.

In two years there'd been no communication, certainly no apology or overture of friendship, but suddenly here he was, barging into her life as if he had some right to. That was hard enough to understand, but he clearly meant to take over.

Because she wasn't certain how much the nurse knew about the conditions of her release, the last thing Selena wanted was for her to involve the doctor, so it was best to say nothing now. Morgan had easily guessed that, and she hated the power that gave him.

Morgan handled the nurse with the gallant good ol' boy charm he used to his advantage, and Selena waited impotently as the nurse set the wheelchair brake and flipped the footrests out of the way. With the woman's help, Selena stood to her feet.

Morgan opened the passenger door, then turned to her. Selena tried not to flinch when he took her elbow.

Her quiet, "I want to go home, Morg," made his faintly smiling expression harden the tiniest bit. No one looking on would note that, but she had because she'd learned well from long experience to recognize that first wisp of storm cloud.

"We'll stop by your place to pick up a few things."

Selena didn't say another word, but she had no intention of picking up anything or going anywhere but her apartment. The ride to her building wouldn't take too long. Once she was there and no one was around to hear, she'd simply make it clear to Morgan that she wouldn't go to the ranch.

If all else failed, she should at least be able to lock herself in her bedroom and climb into bed. It aggravated her to think she was capable of so little, but since she was fading fast now, she was certain to fall instantly to sleep the moment she laid down. And once she was comfortably settled, she doubted very much that Morg would take her out of bed and carry her off. He was familiar enough with injuries and concussions to know how vital rest was.

Selena was forced to allow Morgan's supporting hand as she took the two small steps from her wheelchair. Once she had, she pulled away and tried to get a handhold to climb up into the tall vehicle.

Morgan gently caught her, managing to pick her up and place her on the seat without hurting her. Though she would have liked to object, the rational part of her brain was grateful she hadn't had to climb up under her own power.

Morgan swiftly buckled her seat belt before she could do it for herself, then backed away to firmly close the passenger door while Selena struggled against the excitement that lingered simply because she'd been in his arms a few seconds. She'd actually felt the tingling heat through her clothes when the back of his fingers skimmed across her stomach and hip as he'd secured her seat belt.

After days of hurting and years of secretly missing him, being held and touched by Morgan had been completely welcome and wonderful, so wonderful that she'd have to work harder than ever to keep him from guessing his effect on her.

Selena waited, her head leaned against the headrest and her eyes closed as Morg opened the back of the big vehicle to put her flowers and plants inside. She heard the rattle of the plastic bag, then the solid thud of the door closing. A few seconds later, Morgan was getting in on the driver's side. He buckled up then slowly pulled the big vehicle away from the curb. The effortless movement of the SUV as it accelerated pressed her back into the seat.

Her headaches had been mellowing, but after this small exertion just now, her head ached with a vengeance. That's when the significance of riding in a vehicle struck her and she opened her eyes to uneasily watch the street beyond the windshield, particularly upcoming intersections.

Though the high profile SUV was quite unlike her much smaller car—her totally wrecked car—she was on edge. And though the big vehicle moved smoothly, the growing dizziness the movement caused made her faintly nauseous.

It seemed to take forever to go the three miles to her apartment building, and by the time they got there, Selena was carsick. Reluctant to move even after Morgan parked at the curb, Selena concentrated on breathing steadily as she waited for the nausea to calm.

''Why the hell didn't you say something?''

There was a wealth of impatience in Morgan's growl, but also a wealth of regret that Selena tried to ignore. The good part about getting carsick was that

Morgan would surely see that she'd never be able to tolerate the long drive to the ranch. At least there'd be no need to summon the energy to oppose him.

"You told me never to give the time of day to men who swear in my presence." She took what satisfaction she could in the brief silence before he spoke.

"You're like a cat in the wild that's got hurt and can't afford to look weak. Puff up and growl as much as you like." The blunt words were, as usual, dead on. "How much food have you got on your stomach?"

"Want to find out?" The bit of defiance actually helped mellow her roiling middle. The interior of the big vehicle went silent again except for the muted rumble of the engine and the faint whir of the air-conditioning.

The subtle vibration of the idling engine probably prevented a quicker recovery from the nausea, but at last it ebbed and Selena wearily lifted her head from the headrest and forced her eyes to open.

Morgan took that as a sign she was ready, because he got out of the truck and came around to her side. She managed to get her keys out of her handbag, but when he opened the passenger door, he smoothly took them. She was about to climb down on her own when he reached for her.

Selena braced a hand against his chest to ward him off. "I can walk."

Morgan took her hand and cautiously lifted it to wrap her arm around his neck. "That hurt?"

Selena glared into his blue gaze. "I said, I can walk."

"It'll hurt less to pick you up from here than it will be when those knees give out.'' With that, Morg plucked her off the seat, stepped back, then pushed the passenger door closed with his boot.

This time his musky aftershave scent filled her nostrils and the sensation of being cradled securely against him made her hurting body forget its various aches and pains.

The cotton of his shirt did little more than add a textured veneer over the warm, hard flesh and iron muscle of the shoulders beneath her bare forearm and palm. Selena tried to keep her gaze away from Morgan's harsh profile as he effortlessly strode up the front walk to the door of her building.

She was a flyweight for a man like him, and the stark awareness of his brute-like masculinity made her feel fully feminine and helplessly attracted.

In no time they were past the security door. Morgan, of course, had managed to use her passkey to open the door without putting her down. When they reached her first floor apartment, he did the same thing.

Selena expected him to set her on her feet once they were inside her door, but he walked through the tiny entryway into the living room then on toward the short hall that led to her bedroom.

Her soft, "Wait," brought him to a halt.

"You need a nap."

Selena made a restless move, and was relieved when Morgan set her on her feet.

"After you're gone," she told him, then moved to a nearby armchair to sit down. "I'd be grateful if you'd bring in my things before you start back to the ranch."

Selena heard the impatient rattle of her keys in his hand and she knew the significance of his silence in the wake of her none-too-subtle invitation to leave. He'd not responded to it verbally because he didn't waste breath on what he called "pointless arguments."

Of course, Morgan Conroe defined "pointless arguments" as ones that centered on what he called "settled facts," which was something akin to the legal term "settled law."

And on Conroe Ranch, Morgan's word was very much settled law. That attitude had been bred into him by generations of autocratic forbearers, and made him almost too formidable to take on. But she'd have to.

Selena could only hope to somehow scrape up the strength—and sadly, the will—to stand up to him. She couldn't allow herself to be dragged back into his sphere of absolute rule.

CHAPTER TWO

SELENA couldn't relax until she heard Morgan walk out of her apartment to get her things. Once he was gone, she leaned her head back against the chair cushion.

A year and a half ago, she would have loved to have had him barge into her life like this, but back then she'd only been gone from Conroe Ranch six months. Six months was almost nothing for men as stubborn as Morgan, and during that time she'd still had hope they could somehow be reconciled. She'd never truly understood why he'd continued to freeze her out those last years.

But that first six months had dragged into seven, then on into eight, then into a year, pounding home and confirming the painful idea that her life at Conroe Ranch was well and truly over, and that she and Morgan would be permanently estranged.

It had taken monumental effort to move on, but she'd done it and she wasn't about to let herself think it could ever be possible to go back. Morgan was too harsh and unbending to ever again trust his friendship. If she ever gave any indication of attraction, he might freeze her out again, and she'd be faced with another painful struggle to get over it.

After all, Morgan's out-of-the-blue intrusion into her life might only be because he'd found out she'd been hurt and he'd felt a bit of leftover family obligation to her. She wasn't surprised by that because his sense of family and duty were two more things about him that she'd admired and been in love with while she'd still felt secure in that magic circle of privilege.

Since neither of them had much family left beyond a handful of distant cousins they rarely saw, his showing up now was probably more because of that than anything else.

Even so, why would he bother? She hadn't been family to him for years, not since that time when she'd been seventeen and spoiled everything between them. Her mother and his father had passed away by the time she'd moved from the ranch and after two years of no contact, Morgan shouldn't even have found out this soon about her accident, much less put in an appearance. If ever.

Selena was finally too weary to try to figure it out. It felt so good to simply sit there and feel herself sink into the warm comfort of the chair that she was dozing before she realized it.

The next thing she knew, she was being lifted.

"Oh, would you leave me alone." The plea was as weak and drowsy as she felt, but Morgan didn't so much as hesitate as he strode to the hall then walked on into her bedroom.

She didn't have the physical strength to fight him, and her heart quailed at the realization because Morgan's nearness and attention after so long of being starved for even a crumb of care from him was almost impossible to resist.

But then he was laying her on the bed and she stirred enough to realize that he'd managed to pull down the comforter and top sheet. Her eyelids were too heavy to open so she lay there, unable to rally a protest as he made quick work of her shoes then pulled the covers over her.

As suddenly as if someone had switched off a lamp, Selena fell deeply asleep.

* * *

She'd slept the day away, and it worried him. He'd almost paged the doctor, but when he was able to rouse her and she'd muttered, "Go away," Morgan decided she was resting naturally.

Once she woke up, she'd feel like hell after sleeping in her clothes, but there was nothing he could do about that. If he'd gotten her to the ranch, there'd be women around to help her with things like nightgowns.

And bathing. He doubted she could stand up by herself very long, especially on a slippery shower surface, so she'd need help or close supervision. He couldn't handle that for her either. He'd spent too many years keeping on his side of that line, and he didn't expect to ever cross it.

The reminder made him wonder again why he was here, why he was doing this, but he didn't let himself think too deeply on that subject. The tension in his gut was proof of something; instinct warned him to leave it alone.

All he wanted to see was that he'd gotten a call and he'd been compelled to do something for Selena. She didn't have family who'd close around her at a time like this, so he'd had to at least look in on her. That was explanation enough for why he was here. That and the fact that she might have been killed.

Most of the time, he didn't let himself think about Selena Keith. But the notion that she'd had a brush with death—and if the impact had hit the driver's side door just a little more squarely, she might have died—had given him a peculiar sense of foreboding that still rode him hard.

Though he rarely allowed himself think about her, he suspected it was partly because he'd known exactly where she'd been all this time, that she was making her own way and doing well. Until now, he'd let it be enough to know she was somewhere within easy reach. If he'd ever felt inclined to see her, he'd known where to look.

She was still on that same invisible tether he suspected they might always have between them, but her brush with death had jolted that sense of connection. He'd suddenly known that if he didn't do something to take up the slack between them—and quick—that their invisible tether might snap.

It was a hell of a way to feel, a hell of a thing to want to keep, and it made him restless. There was nothing useful to do in her apartment but wait for her to wake up. He'd looked closer at the pictures in the hall that he'd noticed earlier, seen a couple of himself and felt a sharp nick of regret, then turned on her TV to channel-surf and check the weather and market forecasts. He finally made a few business calls including one to the ranch, before he settled sullenly in her living room to wait.

When suppertime finally came around, he found her phone book, called a restaurant to place a carryout order, then left the apartment to pick it up.

Selena focused blurrily on the alarm clock on her night table. It was 6:00 p.m. She lay there a few moments more, listening, but the apartment was silent. It was the kind of silence that told her she was alone, so she slowly got up, grateful Morgan had gone.

She went to her dresser for fresh underwear and a T-shirt and jeans then walked into the bathroom, pleased that she felt stronger. Nevertheless, by the time she took a quick shower and washed her hair, she was worn out.

Selena sat out in her bedroom on a chair to blow-dry her hair and tried to remember what she had in the kitchen to eat. Her arms tired long before her thick mane of straight hair was completely dry, but it would finish rapidly enough on its own. Since eating something would go a long way to boosting her strength, she got up to make her way to the kitchen.

The moment she stepped into the hall, she heard the apartment door open. Her heart sank as the sound of bootsteps confirmed that Morgan must only have gone out for a while. She'd forgotten he still had her keys so of course he'd be able to come and go at will.

Morgan was just walking into the kitchen from the entryway as she stepped in from the hall. The boxes of hot food he was carrying had the name of a local steak house stamped on the side, so he'd evidently gone out to pick up supper.

The rich, meaty aroma of marinated beef made her stomach clench with real hunger. Hospital food hadn't appealed to her at all, and now suddenly she was starved. Morgan's voice was gruff.

"If you've got an appetite, this'll fix it." And then his blue gaze made a head to toe sweep of her and his neutral expression went stony.

He'd noticed that she'd showered, and it was clear he took a dim view of that. At least he'd kept his disapproval to himself. On the other hand, she couldn't have missed reading it in his face so he'd communicated as efficiently as if he's said it out loud.

"Sit down wherever you want and I'll bring it to you."

Selena felt her heart shrink in self-protection. "Morgan…I appreciate the food, but after we eat...'' She let her voice trail off. She sounded ungrateful enough without adding some version of ''you'll have to leave,'' but Morgan knew exactly what she'd left out.

''We'll discuss it later,'' he growled, and Selena was reminded of how very often he growled or was gruff. And also that Morgan rarely ''discussed'' anything. She wasn't too sure he knew the definition of the word, at least not the dictionary one.

She offered a lame-sounding, ''We can sit at the table.''

''This one or the one in the front room?''

Selena felt an unexpected spark of amusement that she concealed. ''The front room,'' she said, though she was referring to the apartment's combination living room/dining room.

For all his wealth and business finesse, Morgan had a very informal manner of speech, along with a few down-home expressions that only a handful of people used anymore. His big house had an old-fashioned parlor that was rarely used, a dining room, a family room, and a living room he called the ''front room.''

Since her living room/dining room was nearest the street, he'd of course refer to it the same way. Household terms weren't a priority for Morgan, and he had a way of making himself understood that didn't encourage him to amend his vocabulary. And anyway, he hired others to pay attention to those kinds of things because his domain was the outdoors.

Morgan waited for her to lead the way into the dining room end of the ''front room'' while he followed with the food boxes.

"D'you still eat medium rare?" he asked as she sat down and he put the boxes on the table.

Selena nodded then remembered they'd need something to drink. She braced her palms on the edge of the table and stood stiffly.

His low, "Now what?" made her glance his way.

"I'll make some coffee. Or get sodas if you'd prefer those."

"I'll get the sodas. You can tell me how to make coffee later." He opened one of the boxes and set out a cardboard plate of steak and vegetables in front of her. "Looks like I'd better get some decent plates. Where at?"

Selena sank back down, secretly relieved he was taking over. "Plates are in the cupboard to the left of the sink, glasses are in the one on the right.

Silverware's in the drawer next to the stove."

When he went off to get them, Selena eyed the wonderful steak, baked potato and steamed vegetables on her plate. She reached for a pea pod and had a taste, then felt a surprising rush of emotion. Her head hurt, she felt weak again, and she was so hungry she felt like picking up the steak in her bare hands and taking a big bite. Most of all, she was confused by all this, confused by Morgan.

Though she'd been warned that her emotions might be a little precarious for a while, she was stunned by the stinging nettle of tears that blurred everything and made her want to sob. Somehow she managed to get control of them, but the consequence of that was a pounding headache.

Morgan came back in with plates, silverware and glasses, thunked it all on the table, then set about shifting her food from the disposable plate to one of the plain white china plates he'd brought in. He did a surprisingly deft job, then opened one of the other boxes and took out a paper bag of Texas toast slices that he tore open and set within easy reach.

He left to go back to the kitchen for a tray of ice cubes, which he brought to the table, and two cans of soda. Since it would be impolite to start eating before Morgan was ready, Selena fidgeted a little as she waited for him to finish putting ice in the glasses and opening the sodas. She reached for one of the paper napkins he'd taken out and spread it on her lap to keep herself from grabbing a piece of toast.

As if he'd guessed she was starved and almost couldn't wait, Morgan's gruff, "Dig in," was a profound relief. She did just that as he transferred his own food from one plate to another, then sat down to cut into his steak.

Selena practically inhaled those first few bites. She hadn't cared about butter or sour cream until Morgan belatedly reached into one of the boxes to set out little containers of each. When he did, she took one of the sour creams and emptied it on her potato.

Just like meals at the ranch, this one was silent. Because the work there was hard, the appetites were large and by the time they'd sat down to a meal, everyone was too busy eating to waste time on talk until later in the meal. Morgan was also a creature of relentlessly entrenched habits, so Selena was grateful to take advantage of that and get as much of her own meal down as possible before there was a chance for any appetite-spoiling words.

She was almost finished before she finally began to feel full. Morgan was still methodically working his way through the food on his plate, but he paused to watch as she reached for her glass of soda and had a first taste.

"I saw your pictures in the hall."

The low words dropped like a fire-cracker in the quiet room, and Selena nearly choked on her drink. She hastily set the glass down and grabbed her napkin to lift it and briefly touch her lips. She'd forgotten all about the photo collection. Most were of friends, one was of Pepper Candy, her favorite Appaloosa filly. Another was a photo of her mother and Morgan's father, but two were of Morgan.

Though both were evidence of the foolish adoration she'd probably feel for him the rest of her life, at least they were scattered among the others and not placed tellingly on her bedroom wall or dresser.

Thank God she'd limited the display to her two favorites, because she had several more tucked away in one of the photo albums she'd done of Conroe Ranch.

"I saw the one of Pepper Candy. She foaled a while back. I'll bring them to the house so you can have a look when you come home."

There it was. The opening salvo she'd been expecting that would have stolen her appetite if she'd not just finished her meal. He'd bear down now.

"I can't go to the ranch," she said quietly.

"Now that you've had a good meal, you won't get carsick." His brisk statement was a refusal to acknowledge the real reason she didn't want to go home with him.

"That's not the issue," she persisted softly.

"The *issue* is doctor's orders, Sel," he said grimly and she had to force herself to maintain eye contact with the somber look he was giving her. He was a heartbeat away from the harsh expression that signaled he wouldn't take no for an answer.

"I'm not an invalid."

"Head injuries are nothing to mess with. If you're afraid of me, I can bunk someplace else for the next week. You won't have to see me."

If you're afraid of me...

She flinched inwardly and glanced away because he'd hit the mark. But then, he didn't need to use any real intuition to guess that since she'd probably made it clear enough that she *was* afraid of him. Or rather, afraid to be around him. Not because she thought there was even a remote chance he'd hurt her physically, but because it was her heart that was at risk. She made herself look at him again.

"Why are you doing this, Morg?"

"Damned if I know," he growled, "but it's time, Selly. You've grown up, and you've still got your cut of Conroe. Wouldn't hurt you to spend a little time there once in a while. You liked it well enough once, and that won't have changed."

No it hadn't changed; it would never change. Selena had loved the ranch, and she was still too often homesick for it. Conroe Ranch had been her first real home, the first place in her life where she'd felt accepted, cared about, and completely secure.

Morgan had given her that, and what child wouldn't fall in love with everything—and everyone—connected to the place where she'd had such emotional abundance? And yet without her memories of Morgan and his goodness to her, along with a few others, Conroe Ranch would be just another massive piece of Texas, then and now.

He'd offered to keep his distance while she was there, but it was an empty offer. His essence permeated everything, so there'd be no avoiding him, not really. Perhaps it was because she'd stayed silent so long that he decided to press.

"Miss Em and Miss Minna can't wait for you to get there. They made up your room yesterday, and they've been baking all day today."

The mention of Em and Minna Peat, the old maid sisters who'd taken care of the Conroe ranch house since Morgan was a toddler, sent a wide sweep of emotion through her that made her eyes sting again.

The Peat sisters lived to cook and clean and spoil every visitor to Conroe

Ranch, and they'd both spoiled her. Selena still sent cards at birthdays and gifts at Christmas to the sisters, and she received an occasional chatty letter from them that she always had to answer carefully.

Selena gave her head a weary shake. "Why did you tell them?" Feeling trapped and teary, she put her napkin beside her plate and started to get to her feet. Morgan's hand flashed out to gently catch her wrist before she could.

"It's time to come home, Selena."

The soft burr in his low voice sent a persuasive warmth through her that threatened her precarious emotions even more. And it was all she could do to withstand the sweet tingles that shivered through her just because his big hand was tenderly shackling her wrist.

Her voice was a whisper. "You fight dirty."

"I can. When I'm after something I want."

His calm pronouncement was no earth-shattering surprise, and neither was the wild leap of her foolish heart. This wasn't personal, at least not in the way she used to dream it might someday be. This wasn't anything romantic on Morgan's part, not in the slightest.

Taking her to Conroe Ranch was something he felt obligated to do because he felt a certain duty to her. His father had been married to her mother, and they'd lived under the same roof and worked together for years. It wouldn't matter that they'd been estranged for far longer than the two years she'd been gone from the ranch. Not when Morgan felt a responsibility to her.

She was well aware that if news of the accident hadn't brought her name back into his mind, apart from quarterly checks and at tax time, Morgan might have gone on for years more—perhaps for the rest of her life—without ever wanting to contact her or even thinking of contacting her.

Or thinking about her at all.

Selena knew all that because it was the brutal, unvarnished truth. She also knew, despite Morgan's insistence that this was "doctor's orders," that she had a choice. She could either refuse to go, or she could give in and let him take her to the ranch.

Her heart shook with a crazy mix of terror and groundless hope at the idea of going with him, of being with him. It was because of that groundless hope that she realized what she needed to do. Perhaps she hadn't been hurt enough before. Perhaps what she truly needed to forever inoculate herself against Morgan Conroe was to again put her heart in harm's way for one final devastation. She'd got over the first one, so she'd surely know how to get over him a second time if she had to.

"I meant what I said about bunking someplace else while you're there," he said, and she tried not to let herself show her reaction as his callused thumb brushed impatiently against the tender underside of her wrist.

"N-no need," she said, then gave her wrist a tug that prompted him to release her. She hoped he hadn't noticed the small stutter. "I suppose you'd rather not wait until morning."

"You've only got one bed."

"What if I'm carsick again?"

"Then we'll either come back here, stop as often as you need to, or find a motel for the night and try it again tomorrow."

Selena stood up stiffly. ‘‘We’ll see how I feel after I pack my things,’’ she said, and turned away to start for the bedroom.

The hearty meal had perked her up significantly, so it wasn’t such an ordeal to pack. When she finished, Selena sat down in the armchair to rest for a few moments. She noticed the blow-dryer she’d left sitting nearby, so she reached for it to wrap up the cord and put it in her suitcase.

Once upon a golden time she and Morgan been friends, good friends. Once upon a golden time, she’d worshiped the ground he walked on. And once upon that same golden time, he hadn’t minded.

In her head, Selena knew that her once upon a time had burned away long ago. But in her heart, once upon a time was still a last magic wish that lingered on in a tantalizing mirage over a future yet to be seen.

Maybe it would take going back to Conroe Ranch and seeing it all from the perspective of two years away that would knock a little of the golden glow from that sweetly remembered time.

And perhaps it was because she was hurting and weary and in a deeply emotional and sentimental mood that she was going back. It could even be because it was an instinct to retreat to a place of remembered security when you were feeling weak and needy. Though she was certain she'd regret this, Selena couldn't seem to muster the will to tell Morgan no and make it stick.

CHAPTER THREE

THE long drive to Conroe Ranch went well, mostly because Selena slept most of the way. It was almost midnight by the time they drove up to the big ranch house.

Because she'd insisted that Morgan not tell the Peat sisters they'd be coming tonight, there was no big welcome when he walked her into the house.

But the price of waiting until morning to inform the sisters, who lived in the east wing of the big house, was that Morgan insisted on carrying her upstairs to her room. Once he'd deposited her on the edge of the bed, he went back down to bring up her suitcases, then hovered to help her hang up the clothes that might wrinkle.

It was strange and a little touching to watch Morgan tipping a clothes hanger this way and that as he tried to get one of her blouses properly hung. If the blouse had been made of a heavier, less delicate fabric, he probably wouldn't have taken that kind of awkward care.

He was intent on performing the minor task and so slow that she managed to get the few other things on hangers by the time he finished and held up the blouse for her approval.

"It looks good," she said. "Thank you."

Morgan reached for the ones she'd done, and carried them into the big, walk-in closet to hook on one of the rods. The rest could wait till morning, though he'd opened one of her suitcases on the low chest at the foot of her bed and the other on a luggage rack that must have been brought in when the sisters had made up the room.

"I've got a set of walkie-talkies downstairs," he told her. "I'll bring 'em up while you get ready for bed. Shall I get Em or Minna?"

Selena had sat down on the edge of the mattress to wait for him to leave because her strength was waning again and she was eager to get some sleep. "No, I'm all right."

"Still dizzy?" His blue gaze flickered over her then searched her face.

"A little. It's not unexpected."

An odd kind of silence surged between them as they stared at each other, separated by little more than a yard of carpet. Selena caught an inkling of… something…in his somber gaze, something gentle and yet not quite gentle, something that gave her a warm quiver of pleasure deep down.

Morgan was the first to look away and that took her a little by surprise.

"I'll get those radios," he said, then strode out of the room into the hall, taking that breathless moment with him and leaving her with the idea that she'd imagined it as she listened to him walk down the hall and go down the stairs.

Selena stood and turned to pull down the bedspread and top sheet, then walked over to rummage through one of her suitcases to get out her things for bed.

The big house had never felt so full, and yet so…private. It was midnight and the Peat sisters must have been asleep for hours now. Without their chatter and beehive activity, the invisible tether between him and Selena had drawn tight. Suddenly he felt her everywhere, and that's what gave the big house an almost tangible sense of fullness.

Morgan was a little shocked by that. He was even more shocked by what had come over him just now in Selly's room.

One moment he'd been looking at her, seeing the weariness about her, then the next he'd noticed how long and thick her dark, glossy hair was. She wore it parted in the middle and kept it as straight as a board, but she wore it longer now, and it went halfway down her back.

Her eyes weren't just blue anymore, they were the exact color of a warm spring sky, and recognizing that likeness made him feel as good as he'd ever felt at the welcome sight of spring skies. Her skin was pale these days. Partly because she'd been hurt and was feeling puny, but mostly because she wasn't outdoors from dawn to dusk anymore.

Her boyish shape had filled out into what he considered womanhood in its prime. Had she been a filly with that much spectacular confirmation, he'd start her on a breeding program to pass on those spectacular qualities. He'd already be considering the right stud to match her to.

The crude analogy sent a fresh stroke of lust straight south. But he wasn't some stud driven by biology and animal instinct, so he clamped down hard on the smoldering sensation.

By the time he got the radios upstairs, he was so in control of himself that he might as well have been carved of ice. Selena must have been in the bathroom, since the door was closed.

He didn't bother to call out a goodnight. No sense giving himself another opportunity to hear the soft sound of her voice, or chance she'd come out and he'd see her in her nightclothes or robe. He didn't want to know what she wore to bed, didn't want that picture in his brain.

It was late, and the soft light in her bedroom seemed to encourage enough notions that neither of them needed to fool with.

He could listen from the hall, and when he heard her moving around, he'd take it as a sign she was all right. The long moments that passed until he heard her come out into the bedroom made him restless. Maybe he ought to sleep someplace away from the house after all.

But when he considered how powerfully he'd reacted to Selena a few minutes ago, Morgan realized that distancing himself from her after this might mean that he'd have to sleep in Houston.

It was after 11:00 a.m. before Selena awoke that next morning. Except for a low grade headache, she felt much less stiff and achy than she had the day before, particularly after she moved around and got dressed.

When she walked down the back stairs, Em and Minna heard her coming, and were waiting when she reached the bottom of the enclosed staircase.

"Well, lookit our Selena," Em said, then wrapped Selena in a warm hug before she drew back to look Selena over. "She's pale in the face, but that's as much a city look as anything."

Minna was next. "She looks mighty good for a gal who coulda died," she said before she too enveloped Selena in a big hug.

"She sure does," Em chimed in, "and I bet she's starved." Then to Selena, "We've got anything you want to eat, you just say what."

"Whatever you planned for lunch is fine with me," Selena said.

"Then pick where you want to eat," Em said.

"We can set you up on the sofa in the family room," Minna offered. "You might be more comfortable in there anyway."

"What do you want Minna to bring you to drink?"

Selena smiled at the double barrage. "Iced tea, but I can take it in myself," Selena told her, and Em drew back as if offended.

"You'll do no such thing," Em declared. "The boss said we need to baby you a few days, feed you good and see you get plenty of rest."

Selena gave her head a small shake. "I don't want you two to wait on me and fuss."

"Why, fussin' is what we live for," Em insisted. "You haven't been gone long enough to forget, have you?"

Minna piped up. "Oh, Em, she's not an invalid, and she's just like him when it comes to pride. You know they both get worse when they get banged up. Like they've got to prove they aren't human, when you know darned well they've got some misery."

Em gave Selena a searching look, as if examining her for evidence of that "misery." "Reckon you're right. It's best to let them do what they're gonna do, no matter how fool-headed, then wait till they run out of sass."

One of the entertaining things about the Peat sisters was their penchant for carrying on blunt conversations with each other in front of the very person they were talking about. Selena hadn't forgotten that, and the fresh reminder brought a wave of nostalgia that caught her off guard.

A bit too emotional suddenly to come up with something to say, Selena stepped forward to give each women another hug. When she drew back, she got out a whispered, ‘‘I’ve missed you,’’ that was more than a little choked.

‘‘We missed you too,’’ Em told her, and Minna added, ‘‘and the boss misses you, though he’d chew a mile of barbed wire before he’d admit it.’’

‘‘Oh, Min, don’t go tellin’ her that,’’ Em scolded. ‘‘Not when he’s still too dense to have figured it out for himself.’’

Selena tried to ignore the stunning remarks. ‘‘Well, I’ll go on in,’’ she said quickly. Too quickly, judging by the gleam of perception in Em’s gaze. Selena was grateful to escape the kitchen and the sharp eyes of the sisters who rarely missed a thing.

She saw the other walkie-talkie on a countertop as she passed, and realized

Morgan had left it with them in case she'd needed to call the sisters to her room for some reason. The reminder of Morgan's sense of responsibility toward her added to her rapidly escalating emotions.

Selena chose one of the overstuffed armchairs and sat down, but was unable to keep from speculating about what Minna had said.

The idea that Morgan had missed her was painfully tantalizing, but whether it was true or not, she wished Minna hadn't said so. Both Minna and Em had known Morgan almost his entire life, and they were always dead-on when it came to what he thought and why he did what he did, so there was no ignoring the remark.

Or the other one: *Not when he's still too dense to have figured it out for himself…*

But what did that mean, really? You either knew your own feelings or those feelings didn't exist. Morgan was just like anyone else. If he didn't know he felt something, it could only be because he didn't feel it. Besides, Selena couldn't imagine Morgan missing anyone, much less her; he was too self-sufficient and emotionally contained.

Em and Minna loved him and they'd always been strongly affectionate toward her, so they were probably projecting emotions on both Morgan and her. Selena glanced toward the door when Minna came in carrying a pitcher of iced tea and a tall glass of ice.

Though Selena didn't ask about Morgan, Minna spoke as if she had. "The boss won't be back from town for lunch, but I reckon he'll be around later. He's got a fair amount of paperwork to take care of."

Selena smiled as Min efficiently poured her a glass of tea and handed it to her. "Thanks, Minna."

Em brought in a tray of food, including a fat slab of dutch apple pie. "We got homemade vanilla ice cream to go on this pie if you want. Just call out. Otherwise, one of us'll come back in a few minutes to see if you're ready."

Em set the tray on the table next to her chair. "There's plenty of room on the tray for that glass. Unless you want us to move the coffee table closer."

"This is fine, thanks." Both women bustled out in different directions. Em would go back to the kitchen, and Minna would no doubt go off to see to some other chore. They usually took turns checking the mailbox out by the front driveway, so perhaps it was Minna's day.

Selena put her napkin on her lap then managed a thick wedge of the cold beef sandwich. The layered salad was particularly tasty, and in no time she'd finished the main part of her meal. As if Em had been spying and knew Selena was ready for the pie, she was back as promised with a plastic container of the homemade vanilla ice cream Selena loved. She waited while Em ladled a big spoon of it on top of the pie.

"Want me to leave the box?"

Selena grinned a little sheepishly. "This is more than enough for now, but thanks."

"Holler if you change your mind."

Her soft, "I will," as Em went out just managed to sound neutral, though inside she felt anything but neutral about this fresh demonstration of the Peat sisters' solicitous care.

When she'd come here with her mother years ago, the two women had been a little scandalized by the skinny child she'd been. Selena had grown up fending for herself and except for school lunches, she'd lived on ready-to-eat junk food, macaroni and cheese, cold cereals, and peanut butter sandwiches. She'd had hamburgers from fast food joints, but never steak or any kind of seafood apart from frozen fish sticks. Most vegetables and most fruits had been a rarity.

Then she'd come to Conroe Ranch and been staggered by the sheer variety and abundance of food, which included almost nothing she either liked or recognized. She'd picked over her food and gone to bed hungry those first several nights, since junk foods and convenience foods were things the sisters spurned. Even peanut butter was something they'd had on hand only when an occasional recipe called for it.

It had taken Em a good two weeks to figure out why Selena ate almost nothing but bread and dessert. And of course, she and Minna had soon set out on a campaign to get her to eat, coaxing her to try a bit of this and a bit of that, kindly promising to note what she liked and what she didn't.

And true to their word they'd done just that, ensuring that there were at least two dishes Selena liked at every meal. Their gentle method had not only transformed her food preferences, but earned them her affection. She'd been a child whose wishes had rarely been solicited, much less accommodated, a child who'd been treated like a bothersome inconvenience most of the time. The two women had made her feel as if she mattered, and Selena had responded wholeheartedly to them.

The change in Selena had pleased Em and Minna, who'd continued to go out of their way even more to introduce her to new dishes while also capitalizing on her favorite things.

They'd also been particular about her clothes, making certain everything she wore was properly maintained, and they'd ironed even her everyday work clothes. They'd taught her to do laundry and iron, how to clean up after herself and make her bed, but once they had, they'd insisted on doing it for her.

And of course, they'd taught her to cook and bake, letting her experiment in their immaculate kitchen—where no one else was allowed to touch so much as a pan—to her heart's content. They'd found something to praise in her every effort as well as letting her in on their jealously guarded Peat family recipes and cooking secrets.

The powerful pressure of emotion that had plagued her since her accident surged at the memories, and Selena tried to keep them from overwhelming her. She wasn't a lonely, neglected child anymore, and she hadn't been after her first two weeks on Conroe Ranch, but suddenly she was reliving both the pain of her dismal childhood and the powerful memories of the gentle souls who'd helped to magically transform it.

She'd come here hoping Conroe Ranch wouldn't seem so much like the paradise she remembered. She'd been after a fresh dose of rejection because she needed to truly break with the feelings she still had for Morgan and this place. Instead, she was getting a fresh dose of care and kindness that only reinforced the notion of paradise.

Now that she was actually here and she'd had a good night's sleep, it seemed idiotic that she'd done something as self-destructive as coming back for Morgan to again break her heart. Her heart was already breaking with love and nostalgia and the deep, deep yearning to stay, proof that she'd virtually thrown away what hard-earned emotional independence she'd achieved.

Selena realized then that she was again worn out, and that the heavy meal was making her drowsy. Desperate to escape both the drowsiness and the feelings that were roaring higher by the moment, Selena forced herself get to her feet. She picked up the tray and returned it to the kitchen. Em gave her a chiding look the moment she saw Selena carrying the tray, then rushed over to take it.

"You look like you could use a nap," she noted kindly, and Selena smiled.

"I'd like to walk around a little. Maybe sit out on the patio for a while."

"Don't wear yourself out and be careful. It's gettin' hot."

"I'll be careful," Selena said, then left the kitchen to wander through the main rooms of the downstairs.

Selena stayed away from Morgan's den because it was so completely and distinctively his, and she soon saw that nothing in the house had changed. It was as if she'd been here only yesterday. Not so much as a lamp had been moved, or even a rug or throw pillow. The same books were on the bookcases, the same photographs and paintings scattered in the same places on the walls.

It was as if time had stood still on Conroe Ranch, a little like the Brigadoon fable, waiting for that rare magic day when it came to life again. She tried not to think about the other part of that story—that if one of the residents of Brigadoon ever left, the place would cease to exist. Besides, she had gone away and the existence of Conroe Ranch had obviously not been threatened in the least.

She eventually made it out to the back patio, and chose one of the black wrought iron loungers in the shade. The design on the fat, all-weather cushions was new but they were kept outdoors almost year round so they quickly faded and were replaced.

Selena sat down then settled back and watched a nearby pot of flowers that sat in a patch of sun, but it was still too hot and early in the afternoon to see many hummingbirds. After the chilly air-conditioning in the house, the heat felt good, and the drowsiness she felt deepened.

She managed to not see Morgan until supper. After she'd briefly napped on the patio, the heat had driven her back into the house, just in time to miss Morgan's return from town. And since he spent the rest of the day in the den, she settled in the family room to watch TV.

When Em and Minna came in to see their favorite soap opera, they insisted Selena have one of Em's heavy, crocheted afghans around her to protect against the chill of the air-conditioning. The fact that Selena did more dozing than TV viewing was another indication she wasn't bouncing back as quickly as she'd hoped.

Supper was served in the dining room. Selena wished they'd eaten on the patio. Because Morgan was anything but an entertaining dinner companion, she might at least have had the distraction of being outdoors. Barely a handful of words passed between them, and Morgan seemed so unaware of her that she might as well have been invisible.

The good thing was that the frigid gulf between them was still intact so there'd be no chance of getting her hopes up.

More than ever Selena realized it had been a mistake to come here. Morgan couldn't have made it clearer that bringing her to the ranch and tolerating her nearness was a grim duty for him, perhaps even a burden. The sense that he was marking time was sharp, and Selena decided she needed to put an end to this as soon as possible.

She should surely be able to get the rental company at the Coulter City airport to bring her a car. Though it would be sensible to wait until tomorrow morning to arrange it, she wished now that she'd done it that afternoon.

She was certain she could stay awake during the three hour drive back to San Antonio. Nerves alone would ensure that, though the prospect of driving a car again wasn't one she looked forward to so soon after the wreck.

Just as they finished eating, Em brought in a wonderful chocolate sponge cake, along with more homemade vanilla ice cream.

"You can either have this now or wait for later," she said. "Both if you want."

Selena smiled, unwilling to decline and disappoint Em, though she was stuffed. "Thanks, Em. Not too big a piece."

Morgan hadn't indicated his preference, but once Em served Selena, she simply sliced a wedge of cake and ladled a generous serving of ice cream alongside it for him. Minna came in with a fresh pitcher of iced tea and refilled their glasses before both women went back to the kitchen.

But not before, Selena noticed, they'd each cast solemn glances at Morgan as if they were checking his stony expression for some clue to his thoughts. It was a futile check because Morgan's no-nonsense expression gave nothing away.

Selena again focused on her food, but was unable to completely finish the dessert. She was weary again, but more because of Morgan's silence than because she was tiring, so she drank the last of her tea and set her napkin aside.

She rose with a quiet, "Goodnight," that got little more than a terse, "'Night," out of Morgan before she walked away.

It was far too early for bed. She'd told Morgan goodnight because she doubted she'd see him again that evening. Since she planned to leave the ranch in the morning, she wanted to look in on Pepper Candy and her foal.

The sultry evening wrapped around her as she strolled to the foal pasture. She assumed the mare was there, so there'd been no reason to ask Morgan precisely where.

If nothing else, the walk would test her stamina. She wasn't used to feeling weak or tiring so quickly, and instinct prompted her to defy it. The dull headache was still only dull despite the tension at supper, so she took that as the kind of improvement that signaled it was all right to have a bit of mild exercise.

As it turned out, she didn't have to walk all the way to the foal pasture because Pepper and her colt were in one of the small shaded corrals between the main stable and one of the smaller barns. Morgan must have moved them there so he could bring them up to the house, as he'd said last night.

The red roan leopard Appaloosa mare had recovered enough from foaling to look sleek and fit. Pepper's foal was a chestnut Appaloosa with a speckled rump, and mother and son were striking examples of their colorful breed. Selena stopped at the wood rails to watch a few moments before she eased the gate open, stepped inside then pushed it closed.

The mare had taken note of her entrance, sniffed the air, then ambled in Selena's direction. The foal trotted along, stopped a few seconds, then burst into a gamboling series of small hops to catch up to his dam.

Pepper hesitated a couple arm's lengths away until Selena spoke a soft, "Come on, girl" to coax her close. The mare closed the small distance and nudged at Selena, who immediately stroked the long speckled nose.

"So you do remember me."

As if to answer, the mare dipped her head and edged nearer. The scuff of a boot heel nearby alerted Selena. The foal, who'd been inching closer, abruptly shied away to the other side of his mother. Selena knew who it was before she heard the low voice.

"You shouldn't be out here by yourself."

"I'm fine."

The gate opened beside her and Morgan stepped inside. The foal took the new intrusion well. So well that he made a few mincing steps in Morgan's direction before he stopped, his small ears aimed alertly at the big man.

"Get over here, brat."

Morgan's gruff order made Selena smile. The foal pranced forward confidently and nuzzled the hand he held out. The sight of the long-legged foal and the big man was irresistible. Morgan had a certain magic with animals, an endless patience and calm affection that inspired trust. The colt pressed closer, started to take a playful nip of Morgan's shirtsleeve, then changed his mind and tossed his head when Morgan made a low, scolding sound.

A moment more and the youngster tried to rub his head against Morgan, but was deftly prevented when Morgan moved toward the colt's shoulder. Morgan didn't allow the babies to nibble his clothes, rub against him, or any number of other coltish impulses, because what was cute in a colt could become a dangerous habit in a full-grown horse.

Selena looked on, then lifted her gaze to watch Morgan's stern profile. She'd been terrified of him when she'd first come to the ranch because he'd looked so rough and tough and harsh. It had taken days of his kindness for her to realize Morgan wasn't quite as rough and tough and harsh as he looked on the outside.

Watching him now with the foal, she saw afresh the tenderness he was capable of, the gentle care, and her heart took a dismal fall.

She loved Morgan, loved every one of his virtues and sadly, she still loved him in spite of his faults. Watching him now, she realized she'd always love him, however foolish it was and whatever consequences were due her.

Selena was still staring at him intently, still so caught up in tracking every nuance in his profile, that it took her several seconds to realize he'd glanced her way and caught her staring.

The cool blue of his eyes leapt into a fiery gleam and she went a little breathless at the sense he was reading her thoughts. Her stomach clenched with dread, and her mouth went dry. No doubt, he'd caught her looking lovesick, as lovesick as she'd been at seventeen when she'd stupidly told him about it.

No doubt. She read the perception that flashed through that mounting blue fire and knew Morgan remembered that long ago moment as vividly as she did.

"Love? What the hell do you know about love?" The scorn in Morgan's low voice had been a shock. "A kid… nothing but a kid…a baby…"

He'd been furious with her, so furious she'd never seen that kind of fury in him before that moment, though it had remained just below his stony surface for days after that.

She'd felt so ashamed. Ashamed of everything, from her flat-chested, no hips body to her feelings. It had taken a long time to realize that she might have offended Morgan's sense of morality. Though he hadn't said so precisely, he might have objected because they were stepsiblings, though there was no blood between them. And the age difference of seven years might also have been a factor, another big one.

But then, she'd concluded those things because they'd made his horrible rejection seem far less personal. She wouldn't have been able to cope with it otherwise, but she'd probably never be completely certain. She wasn't sure she wanted to know now precisely why he'd reacted as he had.

Selena felt as if her memories and her chaotic thoughts about them had somehow appeared in the air between them like a hologram. Rattled, she broke contact with Morgan's gaze, and made herself focus on Pepper for a few more moments as she struggled to make the mental and emotional shift away from the past.

She didn't have the courage to walk closer to Morgan to pet the foal, so after another awkward moment or two, she turned toward the gate and opened it just enough to slip out.

CHAPTER FOUR

MORGAN watched Selena leave the corral. He absently gave the colt another rub before he followed.

Selena looked better tonight, stronger. It didn't take much to figure she'd come all the way to the pens tonight because she meant to leave the ranch as soon as she could.

That was his fault. Just as her leaving here two years ago had been his fault. Regret had been piling up all day, but he'd lived with it for years.

He regretted how things had been between them before she'd moved to San Antonio, though it had been for the best. Pushing Selena away had kept her from staying fixated on him, kept her from throwing away her options on a schoolgirl crush.

It still bothered him that he'd been responsible for that schoolgirl crush. He should have realized she'd be susceptible to it. Not because he was such a prize, but because he'd had a lot of influence on a kid who'd been little more than a wad of chewing gum on her mother's shoe.

Hell, along with the Peat sisters, he'd practically raised her through middle school and most of high school, so the last thing he could have rightly allowed was to let her fall for him. He'd been compelled to hurt her feelings and permanently keep his distance.

Selena had deserved to have real choices, particularly where men were concerned. He'd figured that once he put her off and stayed out of the way, she'd take other men more seriously. At least she'd have the opportunity, and he'd meant to see that she took that opportunity while she could, though nothing much had come of it. Then she'd moved to San Antonio and he'd expected nature to take its course there.

The fact that she didn't seem to have a steady man in her life yet didn't mean she hadn't been actively dating, just that she hadn't picked a husband yet. He was thirty-one and in no great rush to settle on one woman, much less marry. Besides, seeing to it she had choices didn't mean he'd set a deadline for Selena to marry.

It took little more than a dozen steps to catch up with her, and he saw the subtle stiffening of her shoulders. She was anything but comfortable with him. Her reaction reminded him that he'd realized today that the biggest reason he'd brought her home was to mend a few fences. He reckoned he would have done it sometime, but the wreck had been the catalyst.

The trouble was, he suddenly wanted more than to just mend fences. He'd thought about that all day too.

He matched his long stride to her shorter one and made a try. "Might not seem like it to you yet, but it's good to have you home."

Morgan's low voice had a softer edge to it and his next step brought him close enough that their arms brushed ever so lightly. Selena felt the accidental touch radiate warmly through her, and she struggled to resist both it and what he'd said. But then he went on and she lost the small battle.

"We need to talk."

Selena glanced his way briefly and saw him staring into the distance, his stern face utterly grim. She had no idea what he wanted to talk about, but she felt a strong stir of hope.

Stupid hope. Hope was her worst enemy where Morgan was concerned, and she didn't dare indulge it. She looked away from him and kept silent. Anything she might say to thwart the idea of a "talk" would sound like a challenge to Morgan, and the last thing she wanted was to square off with him tonight.

She didn't want him to have even an inkling that she meant to leave tomorrow until she'd secured a rental car and it was delivered. He'd probably be away from the house all day anyway. She was depending on that because the Peat sisters would be a big enough hindrance, particularly since she couldn't tell them the real reason she was leaving so soon. And if she didn't handle them right, she had no doubt they'd immediately involve Morgan.

She'd been foolish to come here, and she couldn't honestly use a knock on the head as an excuse. The sensible thing to do was to correct her mistake, and the only quick, sure way to do that was to leave. Only this time, it had to be permanent. The idea caused literal pain.

Trying to distract herself by focusing on the corrals and barns and the vast land beyond did nothing but increase the pain of impending loss. Could she turn her back on this place forever?

"I was thinking you might feel like driving out with me in the morning. Have a look around."

Selena glanced warily at Morgan's profile as he went on.

"You can catch up on what we're doin' now with the cattle operation, look over the foals and yearlings. We've got a half dozen older ones ready to be put under a saddle, and a couple three-year-olds I picked up this spring that need some finessing.''

Selena faced forward again, shaken. It almost sounded as if Morgan was hinting that he wanted her to become involved with the ranch again, since she'd always been in charge of training. Her stomach began to knot. She had to be mistaken, *had to be,* so it was prudent not to say anything to this either.

They reached the house a few minutes later, but instead of going in via the kitchen, Morgan gently caught her elbow to redirect her to the outside door to the den. Selena went along, certain now what the subject of that talk would be.

So she'd hear what he had to say, but then she'd have to turn him down. It didn't need to be more complicated than that, and if she did it quickly enough, what he had in mind could be just that quickly thwarted—along with the frustrating sense of hope that threatened her resolve to leave as soon as possible.

Just like the rest of the big house, nothing had changed in the den. The stock magazines here and there were current issues and the PC on Morgan's desk was an update, but only a side-by-side photograph would have shown that to a more casual observer.

Selena chose the leather sofa away from the desk, rather than one of the chairs nearest it. She'd done that to defeat the sense of business the desk suggested. And because Morgan could only have business in mind, he'd initially started to sit in his big desk chair. Once she chose the sofa, he walked over to take the armchair that sat at one end of it.

As if she'd been watching for them to return to the house, Minna bustled in with a coffee tray and put it on the low table in front of the sofa. She took a few moments to pour, then handed over the full cups on saucers.

"Holler if you want anything else," she said before she briskly left the room. Selena took a reviving sip of the strong coffee, then carefully rested her cup and saucer on her lap. As she'd expected, Morgan didn't allow too many tense moments to pass.

"Things have changed, Selena," he said, and she glanced his way only long enough to see the grimness about him. "It was good for you to get away from the ranch and see what else is in the world, to try some new things."

He spoke as if they'd been in a conversation on the subject, and maybe they had, though it had been a conversation without words. She looked down at her coffee and braced herself for Morgan's characteristic bluntness.

"But your ties are here. Part of all this belongs to you. There's work for you, and you're entitled to some say in how it's run. You're the only person other than me with that right, and because you are, you share the responsibility."

Oh my, he was taking the responsibility tack. But then, he knew her and he knew the power of that argument. Selena rallied to deflect it.

"You'll marry and have heirs. The wishes of your wife and children will supersede any claim I have with my small percentage. As they should." She made herself look at him and prayed she looked as unaffected by this as she needed to be as she went on.

"And your father never meant for me to have more or do more. You and I both know that in terms of worth and responsibility, what he left me is more token than actual substance."

One side of Morgan's stern mouth lifted slightly. "In other words, 'Nice try'." He gave her a glittering look. "So I'll say to you, 'Nice try.' If I hadn't run you off, you'd still be putting the biggest share of your time and sweat into this place."

Though she was stunned to hear Morgan openly admit to running her off, Selena gave a faint shrug as if what he'd done didn't matter to her now. She had too much pride to even hint she still hurt over it.

"That's why you need to come home," he went on. "I've never found anyone I like to do your job, and no one's doing it this year. I don't have enough time to do it myself."

Selena was jolted by that. Wanting her to come home because he couldn't find a trainer he liked bordered on idiotic.

Apparently she wasn't the only one with pride.

Selena gave him a skeptical look. "There are some very fine trainers you could hire, Morgan."

"No hired trainer is gonna bring those foals and yearlings along like you do, and you've got a nice touch with the young stock. Besides, I could hire someone to do my job while I live in town and play at being a gentleman rancher, but why pay extra when I already receive my share of the profits?"

Selena might have laughed if she hadn't been so confused by this. Morgan wasn't some skinflint out to get every nickel of value from a dollar. He was rabidly in love with this ranch, so much so that he'd work it for a pittance if it came to that.

That made his remark about living in town and being a gentleman rancher complete nonsense. The only way Morgan wouldn't be living here, or he'd let someone else do the hands-on work and day-to-day running of this ranch, was if Morgan was in his grave. Yet even in his grave, he'd still be on Conroe because the family cemetery sat a small distance west of the house.

Besides, Morgan rarely took input from anyone on the running of Conroe, so declaring that she was entitled to some say on that score was at least an exaggeration.

The worse exaggeration—the lie—was that he needed a trainer he "liked," and he was using that and her percentage of the ranch to pressure her into coming home. The people he hired either did things his way, or they didn't work for him, so Morgan was anything but at the mercy of a headstrong trainer.

The ploy made her angry. He *had* run her off but now for some reason, he'd decided she needed to uproot her life again and move back to the ranch. She couldn't let herself consider that so the simplest thing to do was remove his one bit of actual leverage over her.

"I can get along fine without my percentage of Conroe," she said evenly, then looked away and leaned forward to set her coffee on the tray. "I'll talk to a lawyer and see what's involved in signing it over to you as soon as I get the details of the wreck settled with the insurance company."

It had taken a lot to keep her tone calm and her manner casual once she'd felt the silent earthquake of reaction from Morgan's direction. And why was that? Pride? Because she'd outmaneuvered him? Or because he'd rather buy her out than allow her to just give the percentage back?

If the answer to that last was yes—and it suddenly made sense to her that her offer might have offended him—then tough. She could do whatever she wanted with her percentage and he could eat dirt.

It was a good thought to end this confusing evening on, so she slid forward on the smooth leather to stand. Now that she was tired and her body was stiffening up, she couldn't move as efficiently or quickly as normal, so perhaps leaving the room immediately after her declaration had lost a little of its dismissive punch.

She didn't look at Morgan's face to gauge the impact of all this. She didn't need to. The silent earthquake had grown into a soundless thunder that pummeled the air between them. She sensed Morgan wasn't at all finished with their talk but if that was the case, he was allowing a hefty amount of time to pass.

Was he just so angry with her that he couldn't speak or was he carefully choosing his next words? Neither explanation fit his give-'em-hell style, so Selena stepped away from him to walk around the low table.

She rounded the end but because she was headed for the hall door, she had to change direction and walk past Morgan's chair. The moment she did, he reached out and gently caught her wrist to stop her.

"What would it take, Selena? What would it take to make you come home to stay?"

Selena gave him her full attention and their gazes immediately locked. "Why, Morgan? You ran me off but now you want me to come back. What happens next week? Or next month? How long before you run me off again?''

She pulled her wrist from his light grip. ''We've both got better things to do than play games.'' She was about to move away when he caught her a second time.

''What would it take, Selly?'' he repeated, his low voice a rumble. ''An apology?'' A half dozen heartbeats separated those words from the next ones. ''Then I apologize.''

Selena felt as if she'd been dropped off a cliff. Her knees actually went weak. Her shock must have shown because Morgan came to his feet and his free arm went around her waist to hold her up.

A gruff chuckle rasped out of him and a rare curve relaxed his stern mouth. ''Shocked you, did I?'' That seemed to amuse him, but his expression was only a bit less stony.

Selena stared at him, searching for any clue to what this was really about. In the grand scheme of things, she simply wasn't this important, not to Morgan. Whatever he'd just said about an apology, she couldn't possibly be so important to him that he'd actually bend his hellacious pride and genuinely apologize. After all, it was the very history that he was apologizing for that was the biggest proof of her unimportance to him.

"I always thought you were too honest to use that kind of manipulation." Selena delivered the quiet words coldly, and watched a tiny flare of temper burst to life in his blue gaze.

"You think I'm lying?"

"You don't need me to train your horses, so it's an insult to pretend you do. And the only reason you offered that apology is because you want something from me, though I can't imagine what, other than my percentage of Conroe. And I just told you I'm giving it back.''

She pulled away and took another step back for good measure. ''Do you even know what you're apologizing for? Or did you find that idea in the same trick hat you got the trainer out of?''

Morgan's face was as hard as a brick and as unrelenting.

''I meant what I said about returning my share of the ranch to you,'' Selena told him. ''Then it's done between us. And if you ever hear I've been in a car accident, do us both a favor and stay home.''

Selena was shaking, both from anger and from reaction. She'd never stood up to Morgan quite this boldly before, and now she'd virtually called him a liar to his face. It was the first time she'd ever done that, but then it was also the first time she'd ever known him to lie.

Morgan either spoke the blunt, unvarnished truth, or he didn't speak.

The room around them crackled with tension and Selena felt her knees tremble. She felt weak and her head was beginning to pound. There was no reason to keep standing there, so Selena glanced away from Morgan's flinty expression and walked to the hall door.

At first she thought she'd made her escape. But she got halfway up the front stairs before she heard Morgan start up the steps behind her.

His pace wasn't rushed, but it sounded relentless, and his longer stride overtook hers in the upstairs hall. Just as she got to her door, Morgan reached in front of her to brace his hand on the door frame to block her from going in.

Selena resisted the urge to look up into his face. His low voice was gravelly and quiet.

"I regret…running you off, Selena. I had reasons that seemed good at the time. I reckon that doesn't count for much, but your accident made me realize I could have lost the chance to ever make peace between us. I shoulda said so."

Selena turned her head and looked up into the ruggedly handsome face that was now so tantalizingly close. Morgan's stern mouth slanted a little bitterly.

"And that's just one more mistake in a long row of mistakes I've made with you." The somber look in Morgan's eyes underscored his sincerity. "I know I've got things to earn back with you, but I'd like us to be friends again."

His gaze was startlingly intense and yet there was a guardedness, as if he was forcing those next words against his better judgment.

"I like the way it feels to know you're in the house again. I should have said that, too."

Morgan eased his hand from the door frame so she could pass on into her room if she wanted. As he straightened, he kept his blue gaze locked with hers. ''If you're up to it in the morning, I'd still like to take you with me. If you'd rather leave like you were planning, I'll drive you back to San Antonio, no fuss, though I don't like the idea of you being on your own just yet.''

So he'd guessed she'd meant to leave. It was another little surprise, and she just had time to wonder how he'd known before he reached to steady her.

''You're shakin', Sel,'' he said gruffly before he ushered her into her room and across to the armchair. Selena sat down, defying the telltale sting of tears. Was any of this really happening? And if it was, could it last?

Morgan hunkered down in front of her and took hold of her cold fingers. ''And damn if I haven't worn you out, shocked you…maybe both.''

Selena's words came out in a thick whisper. ''I'm not sure why I came here.''

That wasn't what she'd meant to say precisely. In fact, she hadn't meant to say anything. It wasn't even the truth, or was it? She thought she'd come here for one last rejection so she could finally put Morgan and this place behind her.

But after the things Morgan had just said, she was beginning to think this was what she'd really come for: to reclaim some bit of their old friendship and maybe a bit of genuine closeness.

Even if Morgan never fell in love with her, they'd have a chance to have peace. Peace was a far better thing to have between them than estrangement. Maybe never being able to love Morgan openly or have his love would be easier to bear if they could at least be friends again.

"Maybe you want the same thing I do," he said, his low voice a rasp. "Leastwise, I hope you do."

Selena felt her heart quiver. This was beyond anything she could have reasonably hoped for.

Morgan gave her hand a gentle squeeze and she felt the magic of it to her soul. He seemed to know she was just barely hanging on to her pride, so he pulled his gaze away and glanced around briefly.

"Tell me where your nightclothes are and I'll get 'em for you. Then I'll clear out so you can go to bed. Or I can get Min and Em up here, if you want to shower tonight."

"I took it before supper," she said.

He rose up and released her fingers. "You got a nightie hanging on one of the doors?"

Selena realized he wasn't going to leave until she'd allowed him to do at least that much for her, so she answered. "On the back of the bathroom door."

Morgan walked into the bathroom and came right back with her knee length cotton nightgown draped across one broad palm. The sight sent a peculiar feeling of intimacy through her, and when he held out to her, she took it.

"I reckon if there's nothing else you need, I'll leave you alone. Minna brought up the walkie-talkies, just in case. I'll get around to putting in an intercom before we get too many more years into the twenty-first century." One corner of his mouth quirked.

Selena's heart was beginning to soar. This was the first time in what seemed like forever that the old tension between them was blessedly absent. Morgan's tone of voice and the casual practicality of his manner brought back strong memories of what he'd been like once upon a time—that once upon a time when she'd first come here with her mother. He'd been so consistently kind, gently solicitous and a little tentative, as if he didn't want to spook her.

Morgan took a step backward toward the door as if reluctant to leave, his blue gaze searching her face. She answered the telltale look of concern.

"I'm fine."

One side of his stern mouth curved up slightly. "G'night, then."

She said a quiet goodnight and he turned away to stride out, closing the door behind him.

Selena looked down at the nightgown in her hands, still dazed by all this, still overwhelmed by the monumental change between them that had come virtually out-of-the-blue. It was only later after she'd switched off the lamp and lay back on her pillow, that she was suddenly a little terrified that she might have somehow imagined it. Or that it wouldn't last.

Selena slept surprisingly well, which was an unexpected blessing. She awakened just after 5:00 a.m., and was too restless about the day to go back to sleep. She got creakily out of bed and moved around to stretch her stiff muscles. As she got dressed in a long-sleeved chambray shirt and jeans, she noted that the colorful bruises scattered down the left side of her body from shoulder to thigh were starting to change color from purple to a less intense greenishness.

This was the best day so far since the wreck and she was grateful. After she put on some makeup and brushed out her hair, she found a hair tie and started downstairs.

Looking back on last night, Selena felt a fresh stroke of excitement mingled with more than a little disbelief. She wasn't one to mistake a conversation, but Morgan's words had been so unexpected that she couldn't help the need for some sort of confirmation.

To her relief, when Selena walked into the dining room, Morgan looked up and his flinty expression lightened with surprise. Though he was often cranky before breakfast, there was a gleam of open pleasure in his gaze as he stood and waited for her to sit down.

"You've got some color, so being home agrees with you," he remarked, his voice still rusty from sleep. "Did you decide to come with me this morning?"

There was just the tiniest bit of uncertainty when he'd asked that, and Selena tried not to take obvious note of it. Morgan Conroe was the least uncertain person she'd ever met, and yet she hadn't mistaken the perception.

"I think so. We'll see how long."

She took her seat and Morgan sat back down. He called out a loud, "We need another plate in here," toward the kitchen door, and Selena stifled a laugh.

Morgan's informality in the context of the beautifully appointed formal dining room, with its high gloss mahogany table and crystal chandelier, amused her. If it had been a formal situation with a guest present, he wouldn't have done something as down home as "holler" in the house.

Her amusement eased to a warm glow as she realized he was imposing the kind of familiarity reserved for family and close friends. But they hadn't truly been friends since before she'd turned seventeen. Now they were both full adults, so she had no clear idea of what being friends would be like this time.

Minna rushed in then with a place setting. In seconds, Selena not only had coffee and juice, but also a minor mystery when she caught Minna give Morgan a wink before she rushed back to the kitchen.

Morgan's expression had gone stony because of that wink, but his reaction hadn't fazed Minna. Selena reached for her orange juice.

"We'll drive into town tomorrow," Morgan said after she'd had a sip. "Let Doc Moony have a look at you. Miss Minna can make the appointment for late morning, and we'll eat in town. It's the day they go shopping anyway, so it ought to work out about right."

Selena set her glass down. Morgan had taken command, but then, nothing short of dynamite could shake his penchant for automatically mapping out plans and organizing the people around him to suit his agenda. She didn't protest, because it was a sensible idea.

She'd thought the doctor in San Antonio had been overcautious, particularly because she was recovering much more quickly than he'd seemed to expect. And since it looked like she might be staying on for at least a day or so more, it might be good to confirm her quick recovery.

Because they'd already had more conversation than used to be normal at this hour, Selena was perfectly content to let the early morning silence descend.

CHAPTER FIVE

SELENA had brought a pair of her boots from San Antonio but she'd not brought a Stetson so Minna found one of her old ones.

She decided to wear sunglasses to avoid letting the bright sun provoke a headache. Though she'd rarely worn sunglasses doing ranch work, today she'd be riding with Morgan in one of the pick-ups.

Morgan took time to slowly drive her around the ranch headquarters, pointing out changes and additions, catching her up on the things she'd missed or lost touch with the past couple of years.

When they reached the foal pasture, they got out to see the babies. Morgan didn't always wean foals according to a set schedule, preferring instead to pay attention to their dams' nutrition and wait until the foals' natural intake of forage and grain rose to a level close to what they'd need for growth once they were weaned.

Because he kept track of each foal to best judge when weaning should take place, Morgan kept dams and foals in one of the pastures nearest the headquarters in a roomy, protected spot that had plenty of grass and shade. A loafing shed provided shelter on one side of the pasture, and there was a large creep feeder near the water tank. Pepper and her foal had already been returned here from the small corral they'd been in the night before, but they were on the far end of the pasture in the shade with most of the other mares and foals.

"I reckon in another week or so, we can do vaccinations," Morgan told her as Selena reached through the wood fence to coax one of the fillies close. "And I meant what I said about needing a trainer. It's hard to find time to give them the attention I want them to have. And then there'll be weaning to see them through, and getting the two-year-olds trained."

He stopped and Selena sneaked a glance his way only to find he was staring straight at her. He'd been waiting for that, because he told her, "But no matter how desperate I am, I'll try not to crowd you."

Selena looked away and smiled at the idea that he'd try not to "crowd" her. It was part of Morgan's Type A personality to do just that, so she doubted he could easily stick to his resolve, whatever his intentions were.

She didn't remark, and instead petted a black filly's velvety muzzle. There was nothing she'd love more than to move back here to work with Morgan's horses, but she couldn't consider it just yet.

It was best to see how the next couple of days went. Perhaps nothing would come of this visit beyond an end to their estrangement. Moving back to Conroe to live and work wasn't necessarily a natural or sensible consequence of settling things and being friends again. In fact, living here might more likely jeopardize that.

From there, they went on a wide-ranging tour of the land, and Selena loved every moment of it. She loved this place and she'd missed the vastness of it, the feeling of freedom, even the dangers that made living and working here a challenge.

Morgan chose the better ranch roads and drove much slower on them than he normally would have to avoid jostling her too much. Nevertheless after nearly an hour, when Morgan stopped the truck to get out to open a pasture gate, Selena suddenly nodded off. She roused a bit when the truck was put into gear and it eased forward, but the sleepiness she felt was too seductive to resist.

Later she awoke and immediately felt uncomfortable pressure on her bruised left shoulder. As she reflexively eased away from that pressure, she came a little more awake and realized she'd been leaning heavily against Morgan's warm side. His arm had been resting on the seatback behind her, but now he moved his hand to loosely cup her other shoulder to stop her retreat.

''I shoulda cut the ride shorter,'' he said gruffly, and she turned sleep-dazed eyes on him.

"How long have I been asleep?"

"Forty minutes or so."

Selena lifted her hands and smoothed back her hair. She'd not used the hair tie and her sunglasses were gone. "I'm sorry. That was too long," she said, staring uneasily out at the back patio of the ranch house. Now she realized the truck engine was still running so the air conditioner was keeping the cab of the older model pickup comfortable.

She'd apparently slept all the way back to the house, leaning against Morgan. He must have pulled her over to his side of the bench seat, but she'd never known. It left her feeling embarrassed to have imposed on him. Selena glanced over at him again, and caught sight of her sunglasses folded safely in his shirt pocket. She hadn't known he'd done that either.

"You should have woke me up," she said, touched by this. "I didn't need to sleep this long. And you didn't need to sit here wasting gasoline while you waited for me to wake up. That's above and beyond the call of duty."

"You needed the rest. I only pulled in five minutes ago, so you haven't exactly slept the day away."

Morgan's stern expression was set in its normally stony lines, which made it inscrutable. Selena searched it anyway for some clue to the odd stillness about him, then she fixed on the steady gleam of his eyes. The contrast between the blue flame intensity of them and his darkly tanned skin made the vivid color electric.

And she felt that quivering pull of electricity, as if she was a hair's breadth from making contact with a bare wire. The big, hard-palmed hand that gently cupped her shoulder tightened the slightest bit.

Awareness glittered between them and when Morgan's gaze dropped to her mouth, she got the strong impression that he might kiss her. For the tiniest moment it seemed as if he were on the verge of leaning closer.

Alarm went through her and Selena quickly glanced away. She moved stiffly to her own side of the bench seat, flustered. But then, she might have mistaken what she'd just seen. After all, she'd just woke up and her brain wasn't completely clear of sleep yet.

Morgan switched off the engine and opened his door to get out. Selena opened her door, but Morgan was there before she could step down. Because she was still a little groggy, she accepted the hand he held out to her, then belatedly realized she'd also lost her Stetson.

"I need my hat," she said, but before she could turn back to look for it, Morgan reached in to a peg on the end of the empty gun rack. He must have hung the Stetson there, so he retrieved it then helped her step down.

He kept hold of her hand and Selena had to cope with the sweet excitement and rushing pleasure of it. She knew Morgan didn't intend for the simple act to seem possessive, but it somehow did, though it couldn't be more for him than a casual kindness because she might still be a little wobbly.

And if this was some sort of a test, Selena wanted to pass it with flying colors. For all his claim to wanting to be friends again and needing a trainer, Morgan would have to be at least a little wary of her developing a second crush on him.

That reminded her of what he'd said last night: *I like the way it feels to know you're in the house again…*

He'd seemed a little guarded before he'd said it—as if he'd wondered whether or not he should confess that—and Selena was sure she hadn't misread him. She'd not dwelled on the impression last night, but she couldn't help remembering it now. If Morgan was leery of her falling in love with him, he'd of course be reluctant to chance saying something that might encourage her, which was why he'd seemed cautious about what he'd admitted last night.

It was a reminder that she'd need to be careful, whether she decided to move back to Conroe or not. So what if he'd touched her, that he'd carried her around a little at first, and so what if he was holding her hand now? These things were nothing between friends, and

Selena needed to think of them that way and make sure she behaved accordingly.

It was a tall order considering how her body and heart reacted to Morgan's touches and attention, because it was just too easy to mistake things. The look she'd seen in the pickup just now when she'd got the impression Morgan might be close to kissing her, was the strongest example so far of the kind of misunderstanding that was possible.

In retrospect, the impression had to be the product of a still sleepy brain and a heart that might always have hope. She'd have to be vigilant against mistaking those kinds of things, in addition to being vigilant against letting Morgan catch even an inkling of her true feelings for him.

Her resolve was already being strongly tested, so a few steps before they reached the back door Selena pulled her hand from Morgan's. It was important that she be the one who broke the contact, the one who demonstrated that she hadn't interpreted a casual handholding as something romantic. Or that she wanted it to be something more than he'd intended.

She noted in her peripheral vision that Morgan glanced her way briefly. If this had been a test, then she at least had the pride-saving satisfaction of knowing she'd passed it.

Selena ate lunch with Morgan, then napped half the afternoon away on one of the sofas in the family room. When she woke up, she took care of calls to a couple of her San Antonio friends to update them, and checked on her accident claim with the insurance company.

After four o'clock, she decided to walk to the cemetery on Conroe, which was located a short distance west of the house beyond a line of trees that concealed it. It wasn't a very long walk but in spite of the fact that the worst heat of the day had passed, it was still hot and Selena felt the drain on her energy.

Since she spent a significant amount of time in air-conditioning these days, she wasn't as acclimated to the heat as she used to be. And she hadn't recovered enough yet from the wreck, which added to her mild heat intolerance. It was a relief to reach the shady cemetery. She went in then closed the gate and walked to the spot where her mother was buried.

Five generations of Conroe's had been buried here with ample room for at least two more generations. The picket fence was painted yearly and someone was always assigned to keep things neat and the grass watered and trimmed.

The area was studded with aging shade trees. Perennial flowers were planted here and there, giving the lovely, secluded spot a sense of ongoing life despite the fact that this was a cemetery.

Selena chose one of the white wood and iron benches that sat in the shade next to where Morgan's father and her mother had been buried. Their newer headstones looked shinier than the others, including the headstone that marked Morgan's mother's grave.

Buck Conroe's grave sat squarely between those of the two wives he'd outlived, as if scrupulous care had been taken to not place his grave closer to one wife than the other. Buck himself had decreed that, and Selena had always thought he'd done it out of either guilt or regret, perhaps both.

Reba Keith Conroe would have wanted to be remembered as the favorite wife, though she'd never deserved it until the last weeks of her life. Morgan's mother had died when he was a toddler, and Buck hadn't remarried until years later when he'd fallen for the much younger Reba and impulsively married her.

Their marriage had been so volatile that Selena had worried for years that Buck would divorce her mother, though he never had. Then her mother had become ill, and the two had resolved most of their differences.

Until then they'd frequently been at odds, mostly because of jealousy, and the jealousy had gone both ways. Selena knew her mother often flirted with other men and more than once had secretly met a man on the pretext of going shopping, but as far as she'd been able to tell, Buck Conroe had been faithful.

That hadn't kept her mother from suspecting him however, and her jealousy had made it almost impossible for Buck to speak to attractive women, particularly single ones, without provoking her wrath. Even the Peat sisters had come under suspicion until Morgan had arranged for a private talk with Reba.

And of course, the surest way to put Buck in a bad mood was for his wife to show interest in another man. He'd gone cosmic those times when Reba couldn't account for every moment away from Conroe. At least Buck hadn't tried to use Selena as a spy, though there'd been times when she could tell he might have liked to.

Just the fact that he'd never said a bad word to her about her mother or in Selena's presence had been a tribute to his sense of fairness. She'd only known about their fiery conflicts because her mother often recounted them to her or she'd unintentionally overheard them.

Selena had always thought Reba's guilty conscience had prompted her to accuse Buck of infidelity. After all, if Buck was cheating, who could blame her for cheating on him?

Those unhappy memories would always be ones she hated to think about, and they made her feel restless and emotional. If not for Morgan and the Peat sisters, she would have been drawn into her mother's little dramas with Buck far more than she had been.

And that explained part of why Morgan had included her in anything to do with the outdoors. Reba had hated the day-to-day business of the ranch as well as the roughness and the isolation of the ranch itself, so once Selena was out the door, she was instantly out of her mother's orbit.

Since her mother had been mostly indifferent to Selena unless she wanted something, and Buck was absorbed by his near obsession with Reba, Selena might have continued to be on her own if not for Morgan, and to a lesser degree, the Peat sisters, who'd been masters of distraction.

But her mother and Buck were part of the past now, their lives finished. Selena would ever be grateful her mother had married Buck and brought her here, and she would always be grateful to Buck for not tossing them out.

Though he hadn't been a very attentive stepfather, Buck had been good to her and then he'd left her a percentage of Conroe, which had been a splendid surprise. Or it might have been splendid—almost the very best thing that could have happened—had she and Morgan not been on the outs.

Owning that percentage nagged at her now. After her strong memories of Reba and Buck, she had to think about how that piece of Conroe might effect the future. Considering her history with Morgan and the challenge of keeping her feelings for him secret, there might be problems when Morgan married.

Though she believed in an idealized version of marriage that her mother had never had, it made sense to Selena that eventually the normal exchange of confidences between a husband and wife might prompt Morgan to mention her foolishness years ago. She doubted Morgan would ever announce it, but perhaps some casual remark could give it away.

On the other hand, Selena was not only guilty of still being in love with him, but she still felt ashamed about that time she'd confessed to Morgan, so she might be worried over nothing. Her unwise confession couldn't be something

Morgan thought about very often, at least she hoped not.

And yet she couldn't help but be reminded of what had happened again and again with her mother. Reba had heard others mention the women Buck had dated in the years after he'd been widowed. Though those women had married someone else at some point or moved away, any mention of them was enough to make her mother wild with suspicion. And heaven help Buck whenever one of those women had crossed his path in town or said hello at some social event.

Would Morgan's future wife feel the same way? They'd never dated, but they'd been close friends once. If Selena was working here and living on some other part of the ranch, would finding out about her adolescent crush cause even a sensible wife to feel a wisp of suspicion? Even if that crush was never mentioned, would a wife be alert to any little signal that Selena might unintentionally give off? Since she'd never been able to get past her feelings for Morgan, she'd have to be on her guard all the time.

There was simply no way she could move back to Conroe. She'd never met any man who commanded the feelings Morgan did, and at twenty-four she was beginning to think she either had to lower her sights or remain unmarried. It could very well be that she'd stay single.

And how devastating would it be to watch up close as Morgan fell in love and married someone else? Add to that the idea of seeing another woman have his children and help raise them...

Selena felt sick at the nettle of jealousy that caused, and wondered if she was more like her mother than she'd thought. Whether she was or not, living here under those circumstances would be torture, and it would be pitiful to hang around eating her heart out.

Selena caught a glimpse of movement in her side vision and glanced toward the gate to see Morgan walk through. He left it open as he strode across the grass to where she sat on the bench.

"It's still pretty hot out here for you," he said, then sat down next to her. He leaned back and stretched his long legs out lazily, and Selena's body went on alert when he rested his arm across the bench back behind her shoulders. As warm as the air was, the temperature seemed to go up several degrees, particularly when the heat of Morgan's body made itself felt.

"I was about to start back," she said, though she made no move to do so. Neither did Morgan just yet. He was staring at the headstones, his expression solemn.

"They were a pair," he commented. "The good times were few and far between for them."

Yes, Reba and Buck had also had some good times together when they weren't engaged in their colossal wars. It had been fun to be around them then, especially Buck, but they'd inevitably sink into conflict.

Selena looked over at his grim profile. "I don't think I ever thanked you for keeping me out of most of that. If you hadn't gotten me involved with the ranch, I would have been around for the worst of it." Selena gave a small smile. "So, thank you."

The somber sternness on Morgan's face eased and he actually grinned. "You were something, Sel. A skinny, knobby-kneed city kid who didn't know a cow from a bull. And you were so squeamish you looked like a ballet dancer prancing through a barn lot because you were afraid to step in a little manure.'' Morgan laughed fondly then, and it was a wonderful sound.

Selena felt the sweet pleasure of nostalgia all the way to her toes, but then pain roared along in its wake. They could never go back. Those times had come to an end as irrevocable as Buck's and Reba's, and now there was only the present. She didn't want to think about the future.

``You could have taken sides and treated me like dirt,'' she said quietly, too emotional to hold back the words. ``As you said, I was a kid. I knew absolutely nothing about cowboys and ranch life. You didn't have to give me the time of day, much less help me cope with this place.''

Morgan's smile faded. ``You couldn't help what your mama did and my daddy had his share in the way it was. I could have moved out of the house and kept my distance, but you were an innocent kid, the only one who didn't get a choice. It didn't seem right to abandon you.''

The sudden scald of tears made Selena face forward and rise stiffly to her feet, but the wet spurt down her cheek made her turn and walk with as much dignity as she could manage toward the open gate. She covertly brought up a hand to brush impatiently at the wetness, appalled.

Morgan caught up to her almost before she could wipe her fingers on her jeans. He put his arm around her and the flex of his fingers on her waist prompted her to put her arm hesitantly around him.

He paused after they were through the gate, and when he reached back to close it, Selena used the opportunity to pull away and walk on. He caught up and matched his pace to hers.

"You're skittish, Sel, and you don't need to be."

She was straining to keep emotion from getting the best of her, and pressed her lips tightly closed those next few moments. The intensity of her feelings made her head throb mildly.

When she was sure she could speak without sounding teary, she glanced in Morgan's direction but avoided eye contact. She ignored what he'd said about being skittish.

"I'm just grateful for what you did." She forced a smile and faced forward again, eager to get to the house. "Thanks again."

Stepping into the chill air-conditioning was a huge relief, and Selena went to the hall bathroom to splash her face with cold water.

CHAPTER SIX

WHEN she walked into the dining room minutes later to join Morgan for supper, Selena's gaze went immediately to the crystal vase of red roses sitting near her place on the polished table. And then she realized there were two vases of roses, with one sitting just beyond the other.

Em and Minna were putting food on the table, and when they looked over at her they beamed with wide smiles.

"The flower shop delivered these while you were outside, Selena," Minna told her. "And there's two of 'em—look!"

Em was excitedly wadding the hem of her apron in her hands, and both women were clearly delighted. "We were just trying to guess who all sent 'em."

"Hurry up and read the cards," Minna urged as Selena crossed to the table.

Morgan stood next to his chair at the head of the long table, his expression solemn. Selena tried to ignore him as she reached for the first card. She took a moment to lean forward and inhale more of the rich rose scent before she drew back and opened the flap of the tiny envelope to take out the card. She read it aloud.

"'Hope to see you while you're home. Get well, Lonnie.'"

Minna burst out with, "Gotta be Lonnie Black. He just got the rodeo outta his system and moved back home. Must be thinkin' of settling down."

"Well, shoot," Em said, "he's not the one I thought of first. Didn't think that one had etiquette enough to go to a flower shop and write out a card like that." Then to Selena, "It looks like a man's writing, don't it?"

Selena passed the card across the table to Em so she could see it for herself. Em tilted it a bit as she briefly studied the lettering. ''Don't look like Lucy's hand, so it's gotta be Lonnie's. Says a lot that he'd go write it himself instead of calling in the order.''

''Lucy owns the shop, Morgan,'' Minna informed Morgan in an aside, as if he was some stranger who didn't know who did what in the area. Giving Morgan little reminders like that was a regular thing for the sisters, and Selena stifled a smile at the habit.

But Selena was suddenly aware of Morgan's ongoing silence, and it made her feel more than a little self-conscious as she reached for the second card and opened it.

''This one says, 'Get well, darlin',' she tried not to cringe over that word, ''and let me take you to dinner. C.''

Though it was hardly romantic verse, Selena was sure the message would sound sappy to a man as macho as Morgan. The sisters were thrilled.

"I was the one who guessed Cole Brooks might be one of 'em, didn't I, Em?"

"Yup. But no telling if C is for Cole. Could be Cass. I was hopin' for that cute Jess McClure. He's got finer manners. You'd a thought he'd be the one sending roses. Remember that pretty corsage he gave Selly for the prom? He was always one to send flowers."

"More money, prettier manners, and more serious than the others," Minna said enthusiastically, adding to Em's assessment of Selena's old beau. "And Jess sent roses before, didn't he?"

Em nodded. "They were pink. I always said if Selena moved home, he'd probably give her a call. His mama and daddy always liked Selly. Don't know how these other boys beat him to the roses.''

Selena felt the silence from Morgan's end of the table grow heavier and didn't dare look his way. The roses had caught her completely by surprise. Gossip traveled fast out here so it wouldn't be unheard of for people to find out this soon that she was back for a few days. What stunned her was that any of the men she'd dated would send roses all this time later.

''I reckon we need to make sure we're ready for company,'' Minna said. ''Once these country boys take to sending red roses, it's not long till they start dropping by. Red means they're serious, you know.''

''Gonna be like it used to be, except Selly's old enough now that Morg won't be giving them *the talk,*'' Em remarked.

"Course, this time, they're probably thinkin' weddings, not going to a dance or the drive-in. I reckon Morgan wouldn't get in the way of Selena getting married."

"Reckon not. There're enough old maids around this place, including Morgan," Minna declared, but before the shockwave her words set off could register, she babbled on as if she hadn't just referred to the boss as an old maid. "They quit with that last drive-in years back, didn't they, Em?"

Selena sat down a little dazed by the roses, Minna's remark about Morgan, and the excited energy of the sisters as they chattered on to determine exactly when it had been that the last drive-in theatre in the area had closed. Em and Minna picked up their trays and absently started back to the kitchen, still speculating.

"Yup. Gonna be a wedding around here before too long," Em declared to no one in particular on her way out. "Just you wait and see."

Minna piped up with the last word. "You want an argument outta me, sister. We'd better start lookin' at cake recipes. Remember that one with coconut?"

The door swung shut behind them, cutting off whatever more they said to each other. Selena reached for her napkin and spread it on her lap, still reluctant to glance Morgan's way.

His gruff, "Nice roses," was the most either of them said until they finished supper and went their separate ways for the evening.

The doctor's appointment Minna had made for Selena that next day was at eleven, and Morgan drove her into town for it. As Selena had hoped, Dr. Moony examined her, told her she was doing fine and complimented her on her sturdy constitution. But he warned her not ride or do rough work before she either saw him in another week or was checked again by a doctor in San Antonio.

She didn't ask him about driving, and he didn't mention it. Since she'd decided she couldn't move back to Conroe, she needed to think about getting back to San Antonio. But first she had to approach Morgan about her percentage of the ranch. If allowing him to buy it instead of just giving it back would satisfy his pride, then she'd do that. Anything to keep peace between them while she cut off an avenue of temptation. Or persuasion.

They had a quiet lunch in town then drove back to the ranch. The morning had worn her out, though she hadn't done much except help Em in the kitchen a little before they'd left for the doctor's office.

She went into the family room and dozed an hour or so on one of the sofas while Morgan worked in his den. It was nearly four o'clock when the doorbell rang and Selena went to answer it for Minna.

Morgan was just coming out of the den as she went through the house and she glanced back briefly as he trailed along.

His gruff, "Don't mind me," prompted her to continue on to the foyer to open the door.

Jess McClure stood on the doorstep, still handsome and impressive. He whipped off his white dress Stetson in a show of respect.

"Aren't you a beautiful sight, Selena." He drawled, then stepped in to sweep her into a fond hug. Selena hugged him back, self-conscious because Morgan stood not five feet behind her, watching.

Jess drew back a little and looked down at her with concern. ''I didn't squeeze you too hard, did I? You just look so good it's hard to believe you were in a car wreck.''

Selena heard the heavy stillness behind her and she could feel Morgan's gaze boring into her back.

''I'm feeling much better.'' She gave a little laugh. ''And no, the hug wasn't too hard. Come on in, Jess. It's good to see you.''

Jess gave his hat a toss to the foyer table but stepped out to the porch. When he came back in, he was carrying a china vase with a gorgeous, multicolor bouquet, which he held out to her.

''Thought you might like something pretty to look at while you're gettin' well. There's two of everything, and I thought you'd like the mix. You always liked lots of colors at once,'' Jess said. ''Tell me where you want them.''

Selena touched a couple of the vivid blooms and smiled again. ''They're beautiful, Jess. Thanks so much. Let's take them into the living room.''

She turned and Jess slid his free hand around her waist to walk with her. Selena eased her arm around Jess's waist then caught sight of Morgan's expression and hesitated.

Morgan stood like a statue with his fingers wedged in his front jeans pockets. His face was like a stone outcropping and his blue eyes glittered at her guest with what could only be irritation. His voice was more growl than speech.

''McClure. At least you're more original than the other two.''

Selena felt her face flush with discomfort. She couldn't help sensing a bit of hostility…resentment…something, in Morgan. He surely couldn't mean to have one of his "man talks" with Jess at this late date, not to mention that Jess probably remembered it backward and forward.

She'd heard from more than one date that Morgan had made an unforgettable impression. So much so that despite the fact that her girlfriends reported first date kisses, Selena had never had one while she'd lived here. It was a wonder she'd had any dates at all. But she was twenty-four now, so there was no way to account for Morgan's attitude.

Which was why his surly remark to Jess surprised her. Selena tugged on a pinch of Jess's shirt just above his waist to signal him to walk with her as she again started for the living room. She noted warily that Morgan walked along after them and he actually followed them into the room.

"Would you like me to put those flowers with the others?" Morgan asked, emphasizing the word "others" the tiniest bit. Selena sent him a harried look.

"No, thank you. They'll be fine in here while Jess and I visit. Would you mind closing the doors on your way out?"

Her question was only a little less subtle than actually pushing him out of the room, but thankfully Morgan took the hint. He went out and turned to pull the packet doors from their compartments in the walls then brought them together with a firm snap.

"Where do you want these, Sel?"

"On the coffee table is fine. Go ahead and sit down."

Jess placed the flowers where she'd indicated, then held out a hand to her. Selena politely took it and sat down on the sofa. Jess sat next to her, still holding her hand.

"How long do you think you'll be at Conroe?" he asked as she leaned back.

Selena shrugged. "Another day or so, not long. I have a job to get back to."

"Then how 'bout you let me take you to supper in town tonight? Nothin' fancy. If you're up to it later, we could catch a show. If you're not, we'll just eat and talk and I'll bring you back early. And I know Momma and Daddy'd love to see you, so we could eat in town then drive over home and say hello. Could be like old times."

The offer was a fine one, but Selena wasn't certain it was a good idea. It shocked her a little to suddenly have all this attention, particularly since she'd stopped dating Jess the year before she'd left Conroe. He smiled at her hesitation.

"I see I'm rushing you. I meant to come over and just say hello, give you some get-well flowers. But then you opened the door and I suddenly wondered if there was a chance that this beautiful lady might be interested in going out with me again."

Now he gave her the boyish grin that no doubt still made him one of the most sought-after single men in the area. "Just lost my head a little, Selly."

Selena felt heat surge into her cheeks. "I don't know what to say." Jess chuckled.

"Just say, 'Thanks for the flowers, Jess.' Then you can tell me what you've been up to in the big city."

Selena was glad her refusal hadn't hurt his feelings. They talked for the next half hour before Em knocked on the door and stuck her head in to invite Jess for supper.

Jess politely declined and Selena was secretly relieved there'd be no chance for Morgan to be rude again. She walked Jess to the foyer and smiled when he bent down to kiss her on the cheek as he told her goodbye. When he drove off, she closed the door and started for the den.

Selena had meant to have a talk with Morgan sometime before supper about her percentage, but Jess had dropped by and delayed her. She'd not brought it up that morning, mostly because of Morgan's silent mood.

Now they had something more immediate to discuss. Morgan's behavior with Jess had been uncalled for. She wasn't a sixteen-year-old whose dates had to walk a gauntlet and pass muster. Besides, she'd had enough of Morgan's silence.

The sense of peace between them was long gone, perhaps permanently this time. Since yesterday morning, Morgan hadn't even hinted at the subject of her moving back to Conroe to train his horses. Though he'd said then that he'd try not to pressure her, he wasn't exactly straining to keep silent on the subject, which was just as well.

Morgan's current silence had begun last night, and it had started over the roses. Little more than ten minutes before that, he'd told her she didn't need to be skittish with him anymore. His reaction to the roses hadn't helped her skittishness, but after his rudeness to Jess, the time for skittishness had passed, though not in the way Morgan might prefer.

His behavior was so like the jealousy between Buck and her mother that it rattled her. And yet Morgan couldn't possibly be jealous. This was probably just another time that something had sideswiped his choleric sensibilities. If he ever sent flowers, he had Minna take care of it. Heaven knew he was too macho to actually darken a florist's door in person, so he might have the idea that the three younger men who'd done something he wouldn't do, were somehow showing him up. She doubted she'd ever completely understand Morgan's particular brand of nonsense.

Selena walked into the den, not bothering to knock. Morgan was standing beside his desk, sorting through the last of his mail from that day. She went directly to him and didn't waste time with polite openers.

"Surely your rudeness just now wasn't because of a few flowers?"

As if her challenge had set off a clap of thunder, the air around them pulsed with the concussion. Morgan tossed the pages he'd been glancing over to the desk. His dark brows lowered into a surly frown.

"What if it is about a few flowers? It's what they represent."

Selena stared, taken aback. Whatever she'd thought Morgan might say, she hadn't expected him to just bluntly admit to being upset because she'd received flowers from three old beaus.

"What could they possibly represent besides friendship and thoughtfulness?"

Morgan gave her a hard look. "A single man doesn't send *red* roses to a single lady because he's her *friend.* He does it to make a good impression. He wants to make that good impression because he'd like to have the lady's affection. And maybe a lot more than that."

Selena couldn't help the little giggle that bubbled out. "This sounds like one of your old dating lectures on the wiles of hormone-charged adolescent boys. And what about the ones Jess brought? There were two or three roses, but it was mostly other kinds of flowers. Or was that the FTD Let's-Get-Married bouquet?''

The spark of humor in his fiery blue gaze told her she'd scored a hit on his black mood, but he recovered quickly.

''I'm not saying that. It's just that you weren't home forty-eight hours before they started makin' their moves.''

Selena gave a wise nod. ''And this from the man who can't go anywhere without women throwing themselves at him. How many was it today at the doctor's office and the restaurant? Four? That beats my three, and your four average out to about one single woman every forty-five minutes or less. My three were spread over twenty-four hours, and two of mine got my attention through a third party. Only one actually showed up.''

Morgan's dark brows went up a little. ''That makes my point.'' Selena giggled again.

''What point? What could be wrong with well brought up, respectful young men sending a woman flowers? So what if they'd like to make a good impression or win my affection? That hasn't got a single thing to do with you.''

''The hell it doesn't.''

The words made her do a mental double-take. She got an odd, fluttery feeling inside and went a little breathless. Though it hardly seemed possible that Morgan's reaction to the flowers was actually romantic jealousy, she couldn't help but think about that moment in the truck yesterday when she'd thought he might be about to kiss her.

And that idea was as crazy as this conversation. This could only be about ownership of Conroe Ranch. Morgan's life revolved around this place. It was very possible that he suddenly felt threatened by the reminder that another outsider could be brought into ownership by marrying her. It was as good an opening as any into what she'd meant to talk to him about.

"If this is about my percentage of Conroe, then I already told you I'd give it back."

"What the hell does this ranch have to do with your old boyfriends butting in?"

Selena raised her brows at his repeated use of the word hell—despite his mandate that she should never allow men to speak like that around her—but she went on.

"Don't I have the distinction of being the first person, male or female, without a drop of Conroe blood in my veins—and not married to a Conroe—who owns part of this ranch? I can understand why you'd be worried that I might one day marry a man you don't trust or approve of.''

Morgan's frown deepened. ''If I was worried about you doing something foolish or putting this ranch at risk, I'd have married you myself after the will was read.''

A peculiar quiver went through her and a dismaying rush of old hurt rose up that distracted her from his backhanded declaration of trust. Selena fumbled for a way to recover and pushed on.

''Texas is a community property state, isn't it? So marrying me would have put an even bigger share in peril.''

''If I'd married you, we wouldn't have divorced.''

The fact that Morgan had linked them together on the subject of either marriage or divorce, made the peculiar quiver feel like an earthquake. Selena struggled to ignore it and make her point.

"We're both better off if I give up my percentage. We can talk to your lawyer tomorrow to see what I have to do. That should improve your mood and make you feel less threatened by a few roses."

Her words seemed to just hang between them those next tense seconds, and she watched the roil of temper in Morgan's gaze slowly mellow to simple irritation.

"This is a pointless conversation," he growled.

"It's only pointless because I have no idea why you're upset over a few flowers," she said stiffly.

His blue gaze flared then and sharpened. "You honestly can't figure out on your own why I don't want to wade boy-friends?''

Selena didn't dare say in so many words that jealousy was the only other reason she could think of to explain Morgan's ire. If she was wrong, he'd cut her to ribbons like he had that time when she'd been seventeen.

The two-foot distance between them seemed to shrink. Selena felt flushed. ''The only other reason that might make sense is…is just not possible.''

''Why not?''

The terse question rocked her. Her heart was suddenly beating so fast she felt a little light-headed. But maybe that light-headedness was because they were standing so close and she had to look up at him. She started to back away to one of the wing chairs, but Morgan caught her hand.

"Why couldn't that 'other reason' be possible?"

The glint of perception in his gaze hinted he'd guessed, but he was putting her on the spot to get her to admit out loud that she thought he was jealous. She tried to pull her hand from his but a casual flex of his strong fingers prevented her.

"Why not?" he prompted again. Selena couldn't maintain contact with the sharp look he was giving her so her gaze dropped to his shirtfront. "Selena?"

Emotion stormed through her and her insides churned with it. She made herself look up at him.

"Because that other reason doesn't exist," she got out quietly, nettled by his verbal pursuit. "You made it brutally clear that time. The idea...sickened you."

Morgan released her fingers, but before she could turn away, his big hands settled on her waist and tightened to keep her where she was. She braced her palms against his hard chest, wary of hearing the same words a second time. She couldn't look him in the eye.

"You were only seventeen," he growled, "and you were around me too much to let those kind of feelings go anywhere. I wasn't about to let anyone take advantage of you, especially me. I had too much influence."

Selena shook her head. "That's not what you said," she said coolly and forced herself to look up into his fiery gaze and survive this.

"That's right," he said grimly. "I didn't say it that way. I said you were a kid, a baby, that you didn't know anything about love. Every bit of that was true. What made me sick was that I didn't see it coming soon enough."

Selena's heart clenched with the hurt of hearing the words again, but it helped enormously to know his reason, however harsh he'd been with her at the time. Not every man would have had the decency to refuse the opportunity.

"But you're not a kid anymore," he said curtly, closing the subject. "And you sure as hell aren't a baby. You've dated, you've lived in the big city, and now men are flocking to you like moths to a porch light."

He paused for those next pulse-pounding seconds as she tried to take that in. He seemed so angry, and yet…

His voice lowered to a gravely rasp. "So say hello to another moth."

The shock of those words barely registered before his dark head descended and his lips settled on hers.

That first, soul-jarring contact was tender and warm, almost tentative, and yet Selena felt it to her toes. But then the natural dominance of the man took over and suddenly his lips were invading hers, taking command and making mush of her brain.

A male expertise unlike any she'd ever experienced blotted out her memory of any other kiss but this one, and she was helpless to keep from responding. His arms tightened and he pulled her against him. She slid her hands up his chest to curve around his neck before he lifted her off her feet. He briefly provoked a sensual battle of wills before he again asserted himself and took her to yet another level of sensuality she'd never dreamed existed.

The kiss ended only because he dragged his lips off hers. If he hadn't had her wrapped so snugly in his arms, she would have melted down the front of him to the floor. The world was still whirling, and Selena hung on to him as if he was the only thing keeping her from spinning off into space.

His hot breath gusted across her ear. "Does that explain it for you, Selly?"

CHAPTER SEVEN

AT FIRST, Selena had been too dazed to even nod her head to Morgan's question. Then Minna had called them to supper and Morgan had set her on her feet. He'd let her turn away then, and she'd forced her shaky legs to carry her ahead of him out of the room.

Selena went to the hall bathroom to freshen up and was grateful she had. Her hair was mussed, her face was flushed, and her mouth looked too well kissed to escape the Peat sisters' notice. She took precious moments to go upstairs for a hairbrush, and splashed her hot face with cold water before she came back down.

By the time she joined Morgan in the dining room, he was standing at his place at the head of the table waiting for her, and Em and Minna were just coming in. The sisters set their trays on the table then looked over at her as she sat down.

"Well, looks like you two kissed and made up just fine," Em remarked as she started to unload her food tray. Despite the shockwave Em's blunt words set off, Minna had to have her say.

"It's about time. Won't do for us to have conflict in this house again."

"Lord, no," Em declared.

Selena felt chastened by the sister's rare expression of disapproval. She hadn't realized that Em and Minna knew about Morgan's reaction to Jess's visit and the confrontation it had caused afterward. But as she'd expected they would, they'd taken one look at her and known what had gone on just now in the den. Of course Em and Minna either knew about everything that happened in this house or they found out about it later.

Morgan looked faintly irritated. ‘‘Don’t make so much over every little bit of tension.’’

‘‘Then don’t blow around here like a dark cloud waitin’ to storm,’’ Em retorted as she finished setting out the food and picked up her tray.

‘‘Em and I are gettin’ too old to dodge tempers or run for cover over foolishness,’’ Minna added solemnly, softening Em’s reproof before she went a little wistful. ‘‘What we’re looking forward to is maybe takin’ care of a whole family again sometime before we have to retire. Including babies and little kids, if we’re all real lucky. A passel of those would be just fine.’’

Em chortled. ‘‘Well, sister, it takes something more than luck to get babies and little kids.’’

"Oh, Em," Minna tittered as she finished pouring the iced tea. "I reckon a cattleman can figure out the birds and the bees."

Em gave Minna a meaningful look. "There's a world of difference between figuring and doin', Min."

"Well, yes, I reckon there is. And there oughta be a ring and a ceremony first."

Minna left the pitcher but picked up her tray, and the two women scurried out, leaving a shocked silence in their wake.

Selena's face felt on fire. Em and Minna were matchmaking, no doubt encouraged to do so by seeing faint evidence of the kiss. She shouldn't have been surprised by how obvious they were about it, but she was.

"I reckon your boyfriends aren't the only ones buttin' into our business," Morgan grumbled and shook out his napkin with a snap before he dropped it on his lap and passed her the meat platter.

Selena took the platter without comment, then selected a slice of beef. The sense that things between them were rushing along at the speed of light had already stolen her appetite, and she suddenly wondered how she'd get a single bite of food down.

Thankfully, Morgan didn't say more and there were no midmeal intrusions by the sisters. It gave her heart a chance to slow down long enough for common sense to reassert itself.

Just because that kiss had felt significant and the Peat sisters seemed to agree, didn't mean it had been the kind of life changing event that led to marriage and babies.

And it didn't mean her secret wish for Morgan to fall in love with her was any closer to fulfillment than before. Judging by Morgan's harsh silence now it was more a confirmation that it would never happen. A man in love would want more of what had happened in the den. Morgan was completely unapproachable now, never mind wanting more.

Selena sneaked a careful glance at Morgan, who now seemed completely focused on his meal. She didn't dare keep staring, so she looked away. Selena tried, she truly did, to get down her food, but she was so stirred up by all this that she finally had to give up. When Em and Minna came in with dessert and more iced tea, Selena politely declined both. So did Morgan.

Restlessness made her put her napkin on the table and excuse herself. Morgan spent the evening in the den doing paperwork. Selena quickly tired of TV and went off to have an early bedtime, but it took a while to stop going over it all in her mind.

Morgan finally gave up pretending to do paperwork and walked over to the liquor cabinet to pour himself a whiskey. The sisters had gone to bed and he'd heard Selly go upstairs an hour ago.

The invisible tether between him and Selena had tightened around his insides like a stout rope. Instinct prompted him to fight it like a wild bull whose illusions of freedom and choice were at risk. And now the Peat sisters, whom he loved like favorite aunts, were bearing down on him like a cattle crew at branding time.

He'd been single years longer than any Conroe male before him, so the usual lures of strong affection and lust hadn't yet proved strong enough to get him to settle on one woman, much less make him think about something as binding and final as marriage. He was concerned about heirs, but he wouldn't rush into marriage just to get them. He still had time to be choosy.

Which brought him back to his sense of connection to Selena, and how it set her apart. He didn't actually know what she was thinking, but he'd bet money she was thinking about that kiss and what it meant. Just like he was.

And yet as he stood there in the quiet of the den, he realized he only had himself to blame—if he wanted to blame someone—for starting them down this path. It had begun the moment he'd heard about the wreck and decided to see for himself that Selena was okay. Then he'd got it in his head to bring her home…

For a man who'd prided himself on knowing his own mind, he'd been remarkably reluctant to examine his motives for going this far, and he still wasn't sure he wanted to.

But then his thoughts shifted back to that kiss and he felt his body react. Agitation made him toss back the whiskey and he felt the burn as he thumped down the shot glass.

He didn't want to make a hot-blooded decision about this. He briefly considered whether he was actually obligated to decide anything, but he gave up on the idea of an easy out.

Wild bull or no, he wouldn't just show up at a pen and wait docilely for someone else to either open the gate or shoo him off, any more than he could let himself get roped. It'd be more like him to knock down a fence or two to prove he could, then either cut a heifer out of the herd and take her with him, or indulge in a little basic biology before he thundered off alone to the freedom of the range.

But because this was Selly, he had to watch his step. He had to decide quick whether to permanently cut her out of the herd before some other bull beat him to it, or leave her completely alone.

If he chose to let someone else have her, he'd have to buy out her percentage as soon as possible, take her back to San Antonio, and wish her a happy life. He didn't want to hurt her again, but there could be no vacillating.

He'd give this the same careful consideration he'd give any decision about Conroe, and he'd do it cold. As with the ranch, profit and practicality were the main things. Efficiency was always an attractive bonus.

He refused to follow in his father's footsteps and let himself be dragged along by infatuation and lust. He'd make a common sense choice, and that would be the end of it.

But his brain went back to that kiss, and a whisper of it went through him in a way that made him regret that he'd trifled with Selena even that much. It would be better to never have found out what having her in his arms felt like. Better never to have tasted how soft her lips were, or heard what her voice sounded like when she'd made that helpless little sound that was part surrender, part feminine hunger.

The tough-minded, cold-blooded choice he needed to make suddenly didn't feel quite tough enough or cold-blooded enough to suit him.

That next morning, Selena was torn between excitement at the prospect of seeing Morgan again, and the dismal feeling that last night's kiss couldn't truly have meant much to him. It might have been pulse-pounding and unique for her, but to Morgan kisses like that were surely a dime a dozen. That was just one more explanation for why he'd said less than a handful of words afterward at supper last night and gone back to being distant.

Morgan was anything but inexperienced when it came to kissing women, and some of those women had been so spectacular that it was amazing he hadn't chosen to marry one of them.

A man who'd held out on marriage as long as he had simply hadn't met the woman who could keep his interest. Considering the caliber of the women she'd known him to date, his requirements had to be astronomical. And since she'd known him for twelve years, the list of women he'd vetoed surely included her. Or did now.

Hadn't she come here for one last heartbreak to forever inoculate herself against Morgan? It stunned her to realize she'd lost sight of that, but it was good she'd remembered by the time they'd sat down to breakfast. Morgan was still so remote that he was unapproachable, so that seemed to confirm her sense that last night meant nothing to him. Nothing had changed between them, at least not for the better.

Selena thought about his show of jealousy. She had an aversion to that particular fault, but she'd be willing to bet that once Morgan had kissed her, he'd lost interest in whatever it was about her that he'd felt entitled to reserve for himself.

Seeking one last confirmation of that, Selena cranked up her courage and made a try at conversation. "Will you work outside today?"

Morgan glanced at her, but his expression was closed. "Till about twelve. I'll leave for town sometime in the afternoon."

Then he went back to his steak and eggs, and that was that. Since Morgan's idea of outside work involved riding a horse, she couldn't go along. But it was hard to miss that his mention of a trip to town hadn't included an invitation to go along.

And that was for the best. She'd meant to get a rental car delivered and start back to San Antonio, so she might as well make the arrangements that morning. Depending on how she felt later, she could leave Conroe just after lunch. That way, she could thank Morgan and tell him goodbye before he left for town.

It was better to get away from Morgan's on-again-off-again moods and just move on. She'd done it before, so surely one kiss wouldn't keep her from doing it a second time. At least they weren't quite so much at odds as they'd been two years ago. Her disappointment was even sharper this time, but the trade-off was that they could part on fairly peaceful terms now.

Selena finally gave up on breakfast and excused herself before she carried her dishes to the kitchen. Em would surely have something she could help with to pass the time until she could call the rental office, and maybe before it got too hot she'd slip out to the foal pasture for one last visit.

Em and Minna went quiet midsentence the moment she came in, and Selena knew they'd been talking either about her or about Morgan. She pretended not to have noticed as she put her dishes in the dishwasher, then turned toward the table where the sisters were having a quiet cup of coffee before Em cleared away the dishes in the dining room and Minna started her chores.

Selena couldn't help noticing a lineup of huge bowls on the counter on the other side of the kitchen that were almost overflowing with rising dough. She looked over at the sisters.

"Do you have anything I could help with this morning?"

Em and Minna exchanged glances, and Selena caught a hint of wordless communication she couldn't interpret. Em set her cup down and stood to come toward her.

"Min and I have to make cinnamon pecan rolls and pies we promised to deliver this afternoon. I reckon an extra pair of hands would make the job go quicker."

Selena noted Minna's delicate brows rise high in an odd expression before she too got up and followed Em to the sink to wash her hands and get out a full-length apron. Selena took her hair tie out of her jeans pocket and kept away from the counters until she'd rapidly braided her long hair and secured it. She washed her hands and put on the apron Em passed her.

"So you're delivering cinnamon rolls and pies?" Selena asked as the sisters began getting out utensils and ingredients. "Is there a bake sale at the church?"

Again the sisters exchanged glances before Em answered. "Sel, why don't you get out four of those glass bowls from the cabinet behind you? Don't try to pick 'em all up at once. And no, it ain't a bake sale at the church. Just some paybacks for favors."

Selena had started to turn toward the cabinet Em indicated when she saw Minna roll her eyes then look away with what looked like a resigned "Oh well," expression. Em had seen it too.

“Now don’t you bother with what Min’s eyeballs is a doin,” Em said as she gave Selena’s shoulder a motherly pat. “The less said, the better on the ‘who’s’ and the ‘why’s’ of those cinnamon rolls and pies. You just fix on the ‘what’s,’ and don’t overdo yourself this morning.”

Minna chimed in with, “That’s right, Selly. You’re in the pink again, so don’t set yourself back.”

Selena’s gaze shifted from one sister to the other, noting that both of them immediately looked away and got busy before she had a chance to detect anything else in their faces. Which meant she was out of luck if she thought either of them would give a hint about the “who’s” and the “why’s” of their cinnamon pecan roll project.

Intrigued by the little mystery, Selena turned toward the cabinet and got out the bowls Em wanted. She soon forgot all about mysteries as she pushed herself to keep up with the sisters' efficient work routine.

It was midmorning before the biggest part of the cinnamon rolls were in the two ovens, with pans of more on the counter ready to go in next. Minna had stowed four lemon meringue pies in the commercial-sized refrigerator, and Em was piping a perfectly crinkled and dabbed layer of homemade whipped cream on the tops of four chocolate cream pies.

When Em finished with the whipped cream, Minna helped her transfer the cream pies from the counter onto one of the wire shelves in the refrigerator to chill. Selena gathered up the last of the utensils and loaded them in the dishwasher before she added the soap, closed the door and started it.

"Well, I reckon the worst part's done," Em declared then fixed Selena with a look. "You're lookin' a little pale and puny."

Minna walked over to take Selena's apron. "You go ahead and sit down. I'll bring you coffee and that phone book you wanted."

"Bring her one of the portable phones while you're at it, so she don't have to get up for a few minutes," Em put in as Minna got out a cup and saucer for Selena.

Selena washed the stickiness off her hands and drank the last of her ice water before she walked over to the table and gratefully sat down. Em finished wiping down the counters and came over, while Minna brought Selena a cup along with the coffee carafe to pour a round of the hot brew for them all.

Minna took a moment to get a phone book out of a cabinet and ducked into the hall to grab a portable phone before she joined them at the table.

Selena looked up the number for the rental office and made the call. She barely had time to taste her coffee before someone picked up on the other end. The conversation didn't last long. Moments later, she pressed the off button and set the phone aside. The sisters had listened to every word, politely keeping silent until Selena finished.

"What was that?" Minna exclaimed. "They're outta cars? Land sakes!"

Em shook her head. "Prob'ly not for long. Folks take 'em out and bring 'em back all the time."

"Apparently they don't expect to have any back until Sunday night," Selena said, still surprised. "I never realized they rented so many cars on a weekday."

"They got those weekend discounts, don't they?" Em asked. "Plus, it's vacation time, and lots of folks take driving trips. Prob'ly better to rent a car and put the miles on that. Spare your own car the wear and tear."

Minna nodded. "Sounds sensible. I'd do that."

Em grinned and winked at Selena. "Well, we wasn't ready for Selly to go back to San Antone anyway. Monday'd be a better day to travel. She can miss that Friday get-away traffic."

Minna reached over to take Selena's hand. "And you look like you could use a few minutes on the sofa, child."

"I said she was lookin' puny."

Selena shook her head, wishing she didn't feel so weary. "I'd planned to walk down to the foal pasture."

"Since you won't be gettin' a car today, you can wait to do that till after it cools off this afternoon,'' Em reasoned. ''Makin' that many pies and rolls at one time is more wearing than folks think, even when you've got help.''

Minna gave a firm nod. ''Downright tedious, is what it was. More like punishment,'' she added before she seemed to catch herself. She gave Selena's hand an impulsive squeeze as if to distract her. ''I think we could all use a snooze in the other room. Turn on the soaps while we're at it. Morgan won't be in till noon, and lunch won't take long to put together.''

Selena stared at Minna's innocent expression, certain only that Min had let something slip that was part of some sort of little scheme. Knowing the sisters, whatever they might be up to was as well-intentioned as it was harmless, but Selena couldn't help being intrigued.

The timers on the ovens went off and Em and Minna jumped up to go take the rolls out. They put in the pans that held the last batch, closed the doors and set the timers. Em grabbed a portable timer off the counter and took a moment to set it before she turned back to the table.

"We might as well get in there," Em said, then nodded in the direction of the family room.

Minna stifled a huge yawn that looked remarkably genuine before she added, "Come on, Selly."

Selena knew the sisters were only pretending to need a "snooze," and she suddenly felt teary over that. Once they'd herded her into the family room and Selena stretched out on the sofa, Minna tucked the afghan around her and Em got her a better pillow. The caring fussiness they lavished on her made her feel even more teary, though she tried to conceal that.

Em dutifully laid down on the other sofa and folded her hands on her waist, while Minna took delight in commandeering Morgan's big recliner. Minna aimed the TV remote and switched on one of their soaps before she leaned her head against the chair back with a gusty sigh.

Selena felt even more emotional. If she closed her eyes but managed to stay awake the next few minutes, she knew both women would give up their ruse and slip back to the kitchen. It was a reminder that if not for Morgan, she'd be glad the rental office had run out of cars. She'd loved being around Em and Minna again, and she'd miss them even more this time than before.

But she had to leave sometime, the sooner the better. Perhaps Morgan could drive her to San Antonio. He'd offered three days ago to do it, and a lot had happened since then. He might even be relieved for her to ask.

Fatigue made her set the problem aside, and she drifted off to sleep too soon to catch Em and Minna sneak out of the room.

CHAPTER EIGHT

AS IT turned out, Morgan left the ranch before lunch, so Selena ate with the sisters in the kitchen. If this had been her house, she'd save the dining room for company and regularly take meals in the kitchen with Em and Minna. She enjoyed their friendship, and loved hearing both their opinions and their sisterly debates.

After they'd cleared away lunch, Selena helped pack up their pies and rolls and stow them in the SUV Morgan had bought just for them. He and his father had always provided quality vehicles for the sisters, and this one was no different. They finished and Selena followed Em to the driver's side while Minna went to the passenger side.

"The number for our cell phone is on the cork board if you need something," Em told her. "We oughta be back by four, but if we aren't, I'd appreciate if you'd put that bowl of dough in the 'fridge before it takes over the kitchen."

Minna called out her two-cents worth from the other side of the vehicle.

"An' if you want something to do, Em wouldn't mind if you want to divide it into dinner rolls on a couple cookie sheets. Then I don't get the job."

"Just make sure you wait for 'em to puff up again before you put the sheets in the refrigerator," Em went on, and turned to step up into the driver's seat as Minna mumbled, "Lordy, I'm sick of dough."

Selena smiled and closed Em's door before she stepped back to wave them off. The midday sun was hot, so she went back into the house. She called one of her friends to catch up, then was invited to go out with her and a couple of others to a new Country/Western nightclub just outside Coulter City.

It sounded like a lot more fun than staying in and having to weather Morgan's remoteness, so Selena decided she might as well go along. Fortunately, she'd brought a long-sleeved blouse and good slacks that were dressy enough to suit the nightclub and still cover her colorful bruises.

"I might not be able to stay up too late," Selena cautioned.

"Well, get in a nap and we'll stay only as long as you feel like it. Penny and Darla have to work tomorrow anyway," Deb told her, "so we might all be home by ten."

They made plans for Debbie to pick her up, but then the doorbell rang and Selena ended the call to go answer it. She was a little worried that it might be another bouquet, but instead it was the mailman, and he'd brought overnight mail that someone had to sign for. Once she had, he handed her the rest in a thick stack of envelopes and periodicals before he turned to go back down the walk to his van.

Selena carried it all to the den and sorted it, placing things for Morgan or the ranch on his desk, then taking letters and three magazines for Em and Minna that she left on the kitchen table. Afterward, she went upstairs to make sure she still thought the blouse and slacks she'd brought along would be suitable for tonight.

Em and Minna made it back before the dough rose too high. Since Selena was already falling prey to a late afternoon drowsiness that had finally made it hard to keep her eyes open, Minna insisted on making the rolls. Morgan got home before supper, but Selena didn't see him until he came into the dining room. Em and Minna served, and after they went out, Morgan spoke.

"You've been shut in the house all day, so I thought you might like to see a show tonight."

Taken by surprise, Selena fidgeted with the napkin in her lap. Morgan wanted to take her to a movie? He usually preferred waiting for the DVDs to come out so he could see them at home during the slow part of the year, so it was rare for him to go to a theater.

She smiled faintly. "That sounds good, but…Debbie invited me to go out with her and Penny and Darla tonight."

Morgan seemed to take that well. "Then it's my hard luck for not asking sooner. By rights, you should've turned me down anyway for asking at the last minute.''

Morgan had strong opinions about dating etiquette that ranged from who did the asking, to expecting a man to show proper respect by asking for a date days in advance. Which, he'd lectured, weeded out the kind of ''knotheads'' who held off asking because they were hoping someone more desirable would be available, and then suddenly found themselves facing a night without a date.

A second later, she realized fully what he'd just said. Had he asked her on a date or was he simply trying to be a more sociable host? Common sense prompted her to choose the sociable host option.

''Maybe another time,'' she said and looked down at her plate, ''but it was thoughtful of you to ask.'' She speared a small bite of steak as casually as possible, pleased she'd sounded so matter-of-fact.

She finished her meal fairly soon after that, then excused herself to go upstairs to change her clothes. When Debbie arrived around six-thirty, Em and Minna saw her off.

Selena's headaches had been remarkably mild the past two days, especially today, but by the time she and her friends came out of the nightclub, she had a moderate one. She'd taken aspirin a little while ago, but just walking out into the warm fresh air outside was a relief.

Debbie dropped her off last, since she lived only a couple miles farther down the highway from Conroe Ranch. Selena let herself into the big house, enjoying the quiet aftermath of a pleasant outing with friends. It was only a little after ten, but late by ranch standards. Em and

Minna were always in bed by nine, though it wasn't unusual for Morgan to be up at this hour.

And he must be, because several of the downstairs lights were on. It was the one in the parlor that seemed unusual, so she walked to the door on the way to the staircase to look in.

Morgan stood in front of the big fireplace and was just turning as she appeared in the open door frame. Above the mantel behind him was a large cowhide map of Conroe that had been preserved and encased in a flat, custom-made Plexiglas frame.

The whole room was filled with antiques and museum-quality artifacts, along with several diaries and histories of Conroe Ranch and Texas, which included some that predated the Civil War. Family history had been made in this room, weddings performed, formal pictures done, along with land and business deals. And, though the practice had stopped before Morgan's father passed away, the formal room had also been used for viewings before family funerals.

Morgan's blue gaze went over her from head to toe. "Did you have a good time?"

Selena smiled a little. "The band was a little too loud, but it was good to see Debbie and the others."

Morgan crossed the room to her and she assumed he meant to leave, so she started to turn to walk out when he did. He caught her elbow to stop her and then drew her farther into the room.

"Are you tired?"

Selena looked up at him, trying to conceal her reaction as a shower of silvery tingles went through her. His touch, combined with what she knew about the history of this room sent an odd—and impossible to credit—intuition quivering through her.

"Yes," she answered cautiously, "but not overly so."

He turned her fully toward him and pulled her into his arms. She lifted her hands to tentatively rest her palms on his chest, wary of this. His masculinity was overwhelming in the hushed quiet of the room, and his eyes glittered down at her.

She sensed what was coming—how could she not?—and went breathless. Her fingers shifted restlessly on his warm shirtfront as she detected the solid beat of his heart through the thin cloth. Her heart beat at least twice for every beat of his.

He smiled lazily at her, as if he'd felt that too and took pride in it. "Truly?"

Selena felt her insides react to the velvety timbre of his low voice and she had to remind herself to answer. "Yes..."

But before she could echo the word "truly," he leaned down and his firm lips settled lightly on hers. But then they eased an inch or so away, and she couldn't help the disappointment she felt.

"I wanted to do that again, Selena," he said, his words spoken so close that his breath gusted lightly over her lips, "see if it felt the same." She opened her eyes just in time to see the fiery gleam in his gaze. "I hope you'll pardon me, but one little reminder isn't enough. Not nearly."

Suddenly he was kissing her again, more forcefully this time, and in little more than a shocked scattering of seconds, his lips were taking hers over, swiftly reducing her to pure feminine response.

However potent his kiss last night had been, the difference between that one and the one Morgan gave her now was like the difference between going down one stair and rappeling off a cliff. If she'd had any reason left, she might have marveled that a kiss could be so carnal while they were still on their feet.

And yet only one of them was actually standing, because she'd gone boneless in his arms. She was helpless when he drew away only enough to speak, and she realized she was almost incapable of holding her head up. His lips moved against hers as he said the words.

"Decide now whether you want to hear this or not, Selena. Because once I say it, I want it to happen fast."

Yet his mouth moved too heavily onto hers for her to breathe properly, much less give him an answer. At some point, he moved them the short space to the sofa. Selena felt it brush the back of her legs before she was sinking down. Morgan mellowed the kiss then, and his words seeped back into her pleasure-fogged brain as his lips eased away. She struggled to open her eyes.

Decide now whether you want to hear this or not, Selena. Because once I say it, I want it to happen fast.

Her heart went even wilder as the words made a clearer impression. Selena knew he meant it. Once Morgan decided something and declared it, nothing could keep him from acting. And he always preferred fast action. Hesitating or backing down wasn't in his nature. Neither was failure. If something failed, it wouldn't fail because he hadn't gone after it and done all he could to make it succeed.

That was just one of the qualities that had made it so difficult for other men to impress her. She went light-headed as what he'd said linked with the staggering kiss he'd just given her. Outlandish hope made nonsense of common sense, and she couldn't have kept herself from asking the question if her life had depended on it. Her voice was a barely audible whisper that sounded dazed to her.

"H-hear? Hear what?"

"We can get married on Conroe, if you want to do this in Texas. If you pick Vegas, we could fly out tomorrow."

Little dark dots swam in the space between her face and Morgan's. Selena felt so faint she wondered why she didn't pass out.

We can get married...

The dream of a lifetime, her most futile wish fulfilled. Suddenly. Out of the blue. And it was so completely unexpected that a part of her thought Morgan might be joking. Or was this a test?

But Morgan didn't joke around, and though he could be harsh and hard as nails, he wasn't cruel. And he knew she'd loved him once. Had he guessed that she still did?

"Selena?"

She managed to get in enough air to make the dark dots go away, and she looked into his fiery gaze, unable to break contact with it or say a word as he drew back a little more. He reached into his shirt pocket and when he brought his fingers out, he held an engagement ring.

"Marry me, Selly."

The rush of euphoria she felt blew away whatever common sense and natural caution she still possessed. She was trembling, and then was made more aware of that trembling because Morgan was still as steady as ever.

The gold ring with the bright, happy—and large—diamond winked at her, then winked again.

"I picked this one, but if you'd rather have an—"

"No," she gasped before she tempered her refusal with a much more controlled, "No. It's…beautiful."

Morgan moved his other arm and reached for her left hand. He efficiently singled out her finger and slipped the beautiful ring into place.

Selena had stared at the diamond the entire time, tracking every sparkle and wink it made. The gold band that held it glowed like a grand old fairy tale come true. Her golden memories of this man and this place now had a new treasure and a tangible symbol.

And he'd given it to her here, in the parlor. The place where Conroe men traditionally proposed to their women. The only Conroe who hadn't proposed in this room had been Buck when he'd proposed to his second wife, Reba.

Though breaking family tradition hadn't had a thing to do with Buck's bad second marriage, it was likely he'd known somewhere in his heart that there was trouble ahead with Reba. Since he wouldn't have wanted to chance tarnishing the family record of good marriages, that could account for why he'd proposed to Reba someplace else.

"You haven't said where you want to do this, Selena," he reminded her, and she lifted her gaze to his rugged face, still so euphoric she was slow to answer. As if he understood how much he'd shocked her and that she was only barely coherent, Morgan smiled and the magic of seeing his harsh features go so gentle was mesmerizing. It was hard to grasp what he said next, but she forced herself to calm down enough to listen over the clamor of joy in her heart.

"The way I see it, Em and Minna should stand up with us wherever we have the ceremony. If you pick Vegas, they can see that singer they like so much and we can have the cake celebration after we come home. If you want it in Texas, we'll do it at the ranch, with all the trimmings. The three of you ought to be able to put it together a white wedding in the next two weeks."

Morgan's last words were like a dash of cold water that slowly sobered her. "Two weeks?"

"We're ready, the house is ready, the sisters are chompin' at the bit. All we need is a license and a preacher."

Selena stared at him, round eyed, barely able to comprehend the magnitude of his ignorance about what was involved in having even a simple wedding with a handful of guests, because the words "white wedding" made her think of formality and at least a couple hundred guests.

But then his dark head swooped close and he was kissing her again. She couldn't have remembered her name those next minutes, much less made a decision about anything.

Later, Morgan walked her upstairs to her room. She no longer cared where they married, only that it was sure to happen. Her heart was almost incandescent with bliss, and her body was so sensitized to him that she felt every move he made as if he was still touching her everywhere.

Only because he hadn't been kissing her for several moments did her brain begin to function on some level of sense. It was then that she realized that for all the words and kissing between them, there'd been a handful of words Morgan had left out.

She didn't think she'd said them either, however carried away she'd been, though she couldn't be sure. Although she now understood why he'd reacted as he had years ago to her confession, she was fairly certain that not even a few earth-tipping kisses had managed to drag "I love you," from her. Not until she heard him say it first.

When they reached her door, Morgan turned her into his arms and looked down at her, his blue eyes smoldering as he gave a lazy male smile. She thought he'd say it then. Anticipation made her breathless.

"Two weeks is a long time, darlin'. If you have trouble deciding whether it'll be Vegas or the ranch, remember that I vote for Vegas."

The words were a disappointment that provoked a whisper of panic, but the kiss he gave her blasted that faint panic back to the shadows. Morgan was the one who exerted the self-control to end it before it went too far, and again Selena felt anticipation glitter through her. *I love you,* would be the perfect way to say goodnight.

But then Morgan released her and walked down the hall alone, taking that moment of opportunity with him. Selena went into her room and closed the door. Though she was still so happy that she might have danced around the room, she suddenly felt subdued. The excitement of the evening had worn her out, so that was surely why she suddenly felt as if her happiness was seeping away.

A little panicked by that, she got ready for bed, pushing whatever words had been said or not said to the back of her mind. Selena was asleep only a few seconds after her head hit the pillow.

CHAPTER NINE

SELENA woke up before her alarm went off, felt the ring on her finger, and remembered everything from last night. Her happiness was something akin to joy, and she was suddenly too excited to lie in bed another moment. As she got dressed, she mentally went over every detail, eagerly reviewing it all.

But the niggle of panic from last night came back, nibbling at the edges of her happiness, reminding her that not every detail was cause for joy.

And of course that niggle of panic grew just enough to drag a couple of its friends along. Friends like sanity and common sense, *rude* friends who asked intrusive and completely insensitive questions that made her heart and high spirits go into a slow-motion fall.

Questions which were so remarkably savvy that their answers made Selena look at the beautiful ring with its glowing gold band and its winking diamond in a way that conjured up feelings she associated with all the worst parts of good fairy tales, rather than the best and most happy parts.

And though technically she hadn't said "yes" to Morgan's marriage proposal, she'd accepted the beautiful ring. And she'd accepted it in that room where good matches were proposed and pledged.

Maybe she shouldn't have done that. Perhaps she should have told him no, or at least asked to think about it. The beautiful diamond suddenly felt as heavy as a five-pound weight.

Emotional now, but in a far less happy way, Selena finished getting dressed then went out into her bedroom. She absently paced as she tried to argue herself out of the upset and worry she felt, but the thing that had bothered her last night was now flailing her heart: Morgan didn't love her.

He hadn't said the words, and now it seemed hugely significant that he hadn't. The man who'd lectured her on proper dating behavior surely had just as many rules and picky requirements for respectful and proper marriage proposals.

He might be completely mistaken about how long a courtship should go and ignorant about what was truly involved with putting together a wedding, but since the ideal goal of a successful series of proper dates was a marriage proposal, surely he'd known better than to handle his surprise proposal without at least including the expected declaration of love. To her, love was the only reason to marry.

But instead of following the usual protocol, he'd kissed her to within an inch of her life then told her to pick where they'd get married. Only after she hadn't been able to speak had he said the words *Marry me.*

Marry me. It had been an order rather than a question.

Yes, Morgan issued orders so much that he didn't think about how overbearing he sometimes sounded, but this was different. A marriage proposal was all about a question a man asked when he hoped—but wasn't certain—that the woman he was in love with would consent to marry him.

The fact that Morgan had issued an order rather than asked, told her he'd been so certain of her that he'd not seen a need to waste breath asking the question. The only actual choice he'd given her was whether to have the ceremony on Conroe or in Las Vegas.

He'd been that certain of her, so certain that he'd dispensed with preliminaries. After all, why bother coming to a woman as a supplicant when you were sure the woman you'd decided to marry adored you so much she wouldn't dream of turning you down?

And a woman who'd never turn you down also might not care if you demanded that she put together a wedding in a mere two weeks. His preference for a quickie ceremony in Las Vegas suggested worse things.

Things like not wanting to be bothered with a formal fuss and not wanting to interrupt his privacy and time away from his beloved ranch just to marry a woman who would be delighted to have him under any circumstances. It nicked her pride to realize she was just such a woman.

It would be different if he loved her so much that he was worried he couldn't keep his hands off her, and his haste was instead an effort to keep them celibate until they'd been pronounced man and wife. But lust could drive that rush, too.

And though he'd given a jealous little tantrum a couple nights ago over the roses and Jess McClure's visit, that didn't mean his cranky display had been about anything more than some arrogant sense of entitlement or possessiveness.

Selena was more certain by the moment that Morgan had given her this ring because of possessiveness and maybe lust, rather than love. Morgan was a cattleman whose stock carried a brand. Even his ranch vehicles had a sign on the door.

If you wanted the world to know a woman belonged to you so you wouldn't have to "wade boyfriends," you didn't put a brand on her or hang a sign around her neck. You bought her an engagement ring.

Add to that the fact that Morgan was very competitive. How like him to be impatient with the idea of a normal courtship where flowers and dates were expected, particularly when he might have to compete for a woman's time. Not that he couldn't compete and hope to win hands down, but because he was too arrogant to bother entering a contest whose outcome he didn't doubt, with men he didn't consider equals.

And there was also Morgan's penchant for efficiency. It was always more efficient to go straight to the goal and decisively trounce the competition so he could move on to a new challenge.

Selena didn't want to be another challenge met. Past victories, particularly ones that came too easy, were usually ones that didn't linger long in memory. They were like little trophies set on a shelf somewhere and left to gather dust.

Or was she making too much of this? Had she simply panicked because everything had happened so fast?

She'd loved Morgan so long. Being engaged to him was her fondest dream come true. The freedom to love him openly, to have his children, and to share his life in a way that no one else ever would was the zenith of everything she'd craved but believed she'd never have.

And now all that was so close she could almost taste it. She *had* tasted a little of it last night when she'd gone wild in his arms. But he hadn't said a word to her about love. Because he hadn't, she was thankful now that she'd been too taken by surprise and overwhelmed to say the words herself.

Selena finally made herself go downstairs, still not certain what to think. It was after 6:00 a.m., and she was tardy enough now that Em and Minna would have noticed. She briefly paused to look down again at the beautiful ring, then clenched her fingers and dropped her hand to force it out of her sight.

Morgan was seated at the head of the table when she walked in. He glanced over at her and rose politely to his feet. His blue eyes held a sparkling welcome that eased a little of her doubt. He bent down for a kiss after he'd seated her, but it was cool and brief before he drew back and sat down.

Selena looked over at his rugged face and saw how relaxed he looked. His usual stern expression was gentler, as if he were in a good mood. It wasn't his usual prebreakfast demeanor, and she couldn't miss the difference.

She felt like a ninny. Everything Morgan had ever done, he'd done with the best intentions, even if he'd not always done those things in the best or most tactful ways. Could he truly have taken her feelings for him so for granted that he'd not bother to ask her a "Will you marry me?" question?

Or could Morgan Conroe have a small bit of vulnerability mixed into his macho core? Something that wouldn't let him come as a supplicant to any woman he might have chosen to marry? Yes, he was a proud man, but pride was often a cover for vulnerability.

Her heart picked up speed as she considered that as a possibility. She finally stopped fretting. He'd chosen to marry her, so he apparently cared for her much more strongly than he had for any woman before her. Whether he loved her already or felt something strong that might one day become love, she had to let the question go.

He'd given her that ring last night in the room where generations of his family had pledged to good marriages and gone on to live them. His observance of that tradition seemed to express both his hope for a good marriage and his determination to have one.

Em and Minna came in with the food and coffee then.

"Well, there she is," Em said. "We were wonderin' if you'd had too late a night with the girls."

Selena was even more aware of the big ring on her finger and sent a glance Morgan's way as the sisters set their trays on the table. By rights, they needed to announce their engagement to Em and Minna as soon as possible. Whether they married here or in Vegas, the two women would need every moment of time between now and the ceremony to prepare.

And there were probably only moments before either Em or Minna caught sight of the big diamond, unless she purposely kept it hidden on her lap.

Morgan's stern mouth curved faintly, his low voice carrying a message just for her. "Now or later. Your choice."

Anxiety got her by the throat. Although she'd just decided to give up on the question of whether or not Morgan loved her, this was truly the point of no return. Once they told the Peat sisters, marriage was as certain as if they'd just said "I do," because the two women would never hear of anything less.

Selena toyed with the ring under cover of the table as she debated. She loved Morgan, she wanted to marry him. Did it truly matter if he hadn't said the words to her yet? They certainly wouldn't come between now and the end of this meal, and might not for days. Or even weeks or months. Her heart was committed to him forever, whatever he felt for her. She gave Morgan a nod then felt her tension and the last of her worries vanish.

"Now is fine. Go ahead."

Morgan reached toward Selena and she lifted her left hand from beneath the table to put her fingers in his. He rested the back of his hand on the table to cradle hers so the diamond ring was plainly visible. Em and Minna glanced over at the movement, then did double-takes.

Selena felt a smile burst up at the look of shock on their faces and she looked over briefly at Morgan. His gaze was mellow and warm as he looked fondly at the sisters and waited for them to react. A tenderly affectionate, teasing light came into his eyes though his expression was playfully stern as he said, "You ladies better have that cake recipe picked out.''

Selena's gaze flew to see the sisters' reaction, and she felt a swift return of last night's excitement as she watched it come into their faces.

Em didn't move for a moment, still staring at their clasped hands. Minna was still staring too, and they both were round-eyed. Minna had been about to pour Morgan's coffee, but her arm seemed to give out and the coffee carafe thumped to the table.

''Land…sakes,'' Minna said with wonder.

Em had reached down to the hem of her apron and was now absently wadding it as she stared at the ring as if she couldn't quite take it in. Her voice was a hushed whisper. ''Lordy, would you look at that rock.''

Em dropped her apron hem, turned to grab Minna in a wild hug that almost lifted the smaller woman off her feet. It seemed to snap Minna out of her shock and she hugged her sister back, both women giggling with glee. Then they released each other and rushed around the table.

Morgan and Selena stood to their feet in time for Em to throw her arms around Morgan while Minna grabbed Selena and hugged her hard. Then both women switched places for a new round of hugs and congratulations.

"Imagine that!" Em said, still so excited she seemed at a loss for words as she drew back. Minna was shaking her head, saying, "Lord a'mercy, the boss and Selly."

Em gave Morgan's shoulder a stout thump. "Morgan ain't one to dither."

"He sure ain't," Minna agreed.

Then there was another round of exuberant hugs with tradeoffs to spread the hugs evenly between Selena and Morgan. Selena couldn't help laughing at their delight, but when the sisters were done this time, Selena wasn't the only teary one.

Em happened to notice the food she'd just set out. "Well, now the food's gone cold. We need to warm it up."

Morgan stopped her. "The food's fine, Miss Em. What's left is to get Selena to decide where we're gonna do this. We want you and Miss Min to stand up with us, wherever she chooses."

Minna was dabbing her eyes with her apron. "Oh, my. We'd be purely honored to do that."

Em put her hands on her hips, ready to get down to business. "So what're the choices?"

"In Vegas this weekend, or on Conroe in two weeks," Morgan told them.

Minna gasped and clapped a hand over her mouth before she leaned toward Em and said excitedly, "We could see Wayne Newton if we go to Vegas." Em snorted and elbowed her.

"We can see Wayne Newton later." Then to Selena, "She's jokin', Selena. Just pick what you want."

All three sets of eyes were on her expectantly and Selena suddenly felt more teary than ever. Her voice was a little choked.

"Morgan doesn't realize how short two weeks are, but I'd like to do it here."

Em waved that off. "What Min and I can't get done, the boss'll hire, since he's the one in such an all-fired hurry. All you gotta worry about is gettin' the license, findin' a dress, and dressin' your bridesmaids, if you want 'em. Course, the printer'll have to rush us some invites so we can get 'em addressed by Monday to go in the mail."

"This is so much to expect of you," Selena said doubtfully, not wanting to cause them such a huge headache. "Four weeks would be much more sensible."

Minna spoke up. "Bein' sensible ain't so great sometimes, Selena. And all it is, is just a big party with more expensive clothes."

Em went on to confirm that idea. "The boss's got a checkbook, and we know just about everybody who does anything around here. He'll take care of the preacher, Lucy and her daughter can do the flowers and decorate the house, we'll do the cake…"

The sisters rapid-fire plans made it all seem not only possible, but doable. By the time Selena sat down to actually try to eat, her stomach was in knots. The first thing on Em's list was for the three of them to go to the bridal shop in Coulter City for a dress, which they'd do as soon as the shop opened. Em had declared that if they didn't find one good enough there, they'd go straight to San Antonio.

Morgan was completely unruffled by it all, and had no problems with his appetite. When Selena looked over at him again, his blue eyes were twinkling at her, and she realized she'd never seen him look quite so content. Or handsome.

The dress Selena and the sisters found that morning was elegant and old-fashioned looking, with lace and seed pearls, including a beautiful veil seeded with more tiny pearls that fell from a Spanish-style comb that was encrusted with ever more seed pearls.

The printer could indeed come up with formal invitations on short notice over the weekend—for a price—and they could be delivered by Sunday night so she could address them and take them along to mail on Monday when she and Morgan went to get the license. Lucy from the flower shop brought her order books to the ranch that Sunday after church, and from there, the house had a steady stream of people dropping by.

The Peat sister whirlwind that took over Selena's life included a quick trip to San Antonio that next week to officially quit her job. She hated to do it without notice, but time wasn't something she had the luxury of anymore. She and Morgan brought her plants and flowers back to the ranch, but dealing with the bulk of her belongings and furniture would have to wait until they got back from their honeymoon.

Aside from the trip to San Antonio, Selena rarely saw Morgan, and she couldn't help her disappointment. The few times they got a moment alone together didn't allow for much conversation, mainly because Morgan's kisses were hard to turn down. Em and Minna had given Morgan his own list of chores to get done, so theoretically he'd taken those things on while he'd continued to run the ranch, including a business trip he couldn't put off.

Selena vetoed the idea of bridesmaids. There was enough to do and enough schedules to work around that she decided bringing in two or more others—which would then have to be balanced out by an equal number of groomsmen—would add a whole new depth of insanity to the hasty plans that were actually beginning to come together.

The night before the wedding arrived just as they'd decided everything was ready. After they'd gone through a rehearsal of the ceremony with the minister beneath the canopy that had been erected across the back patio, Morgan drove the four of them into Coulter City for supper with the minister and his wife.

By the time they arrived home, Em and Minna were officially banned from kitchen duties or work of any kind. The cook from the Conroe cookhouse would bring in breakfast that next morning. All the sisters had to do now was get themselves ready and help Selena with her dress.

Because of the arrangements Morgan had made for the noon barbecue, this would mark the first time that anyone but Selena had been given complete access to the big kitchen. Both women, particularly Em, seemed to be taking it surprisingly well, particularly once they realized they'd rather participate as the family members they were, rather than protect their territory.

Earlier in the day, the sisters had moved a few of their things into the upstairs bedrooms between Selena's bedroom and Morgan's bedroom. Mainly for convenience, since it would be a morning wedding, but also as Em had declared, "For propriety and tradition."

Em and Minna were determined to keep all the little traditions, such as the bride and groom not seeing each other before the ceremony, the something-old-something-new, something-borrowed-something-blue one, along with others.

They both came into Selena's room after she and Morgan had said goodnight. What started out as a last minute review of their various lists soon became an occasion for sentiment as the Selena gave them the specially ordered gifts she'd picked up for them on a solo trip to San Antonio.

The two of them gave her a gorgeous locket with little photo compartments. Her birthstone and Morgan's were mounted in side-by-side settings in the center of the elaborately filigreed heart that must have cost a small fortune.

Selena had given each of them mother's rings with their birthstones set between birthstones for her and Morgan, which made the exchange descend rapidly into tears, loving hugs and laughter. When they finally mopped their faces, Em grew solemn and earnest.

"Minna and I are glad you and Morgan are doin' this now, Selly. Before too many more years went by."

"Yes," Minna said quietly. "You two shoulda done it years ago, since it was plain you two were meant to be. We was always afraid you'd wait too long like we did, and miss your chance forever.''

‘‘Oh, Min,'' Em scoffed gently. ‘‘This ain't the time to go tellin' that.''

‘‘Telling what?'' Selena asked, intrigued.

Minna clearly wanted to talk about whatever it was, so she ignored Em. ‘‘Em and I had sweethearts when we were young. Em's got killed. Mine asked me to marry him, but our daddy didn't like him, so I didn't. It was years before Em stopped rejecting every man who didn't measure up to Joe, and years before I stopped lettin' daddy turn thumbs down on any man I was interested in.''

Em had given up her objection to Minna confiding this, and added, ‘‘By then, our prospects were too thin to make a bowl of soup.''

Minna concluded with, ‘‘So here we are, old maids. We were beginning to think we'd passed it on to Morgan, since he's gone single years longer than he ought to have. Course, it's different for a man.''

Em reached over to briefly give Selena's hand a motherly squeeze. ''No offense, but we was worried about you. I was afraid you'd got it in your head that no man but Morgan'd do.''

''And then we got a lucky chance to see the two of you happy, so we—''

Minna's words were cut off abruptly when Em suddenly jerked a hand up to cover a loud cough. The gesture caught Selena's attention because the cough sounded completely faked.

And it had the desired effect because Minna faltered a couple seconds before she went on. ''So…so we—so *we're* glad you both woke up to it.''

Minna's quick glance at Em seemed to seek her approval, confirming the idea that Em's cough had been a signal. Selena couldn't help being curious over another little mystery.

As if she knew that and wanted to forestall more questions, Em slapped her hands on her thighs. "Well, I reckon we all need to get some sleep. Just about everybody we sent invites to has called to say they don't mind comin' to a ten o'clock wedding in the heat. We'll see if those knucklehead Swisher brothers have learned yet how to barbecue a prime piece of beef."

"Yeah," Minna said and rolled her eyes, "we can only hope they counted out enough steaks."

"Don't know why they wouldn't do briskets in their smoker," Em groused. "Folks can barbecue their own steaks in their own backyards."

Em was already chafing at the idea that the food for the wedding barbecue was being prepared by people Morgan had hired, rather than her and Minna. But perhaps more because the Swisher brothers would have unlimited access to their kitchen when they weren't outside cooking over the big grates of the portable steel barbecue they'd hauled in to set up out past the patio that afternoon.

"Now, sister, we promised Morgan we wouldn't complain over whoever he picked."

"But it don't change the fact that it's the Swisher brothers," Em argued as she stood up.

Selena grinned at that. She remembered Em's and Minna's frequent complaints about Sarge and Dooley Swisher. She was surprised to hear they were still around, still cooking for barbecues when they weren't working on their small ranch on the other side of Coulter City.

"Well, if having to put up with those range Romeos is the price for Morgan and Selena gettin' hitched, then I reckon we can stand 'em for a day," Minna said as she too stood up.

After another round of hugs, the sisters went off to their rooms. Selena got ready for bed, then laid there a long time, so excited she was amazed to be able to sleep at all.

CHAPTER TEN

MORGAN'S patience with the fuss and hoorah of the morning ceremony had worn thin by the time he found himself still standing near the house at the back of the seated crowd waiting for Em or Minna to show. They were already five minutes late getting started. He felt a gust of relief when he caught sight of Minna through the sliding glass doors of the kitchen.

The sisters had insisted on having the crowd seated facing away from the house to allow Selena to simply walk out of the kitchen and up the aisle, rather than having her go all the way out into the hot sun to walk up the aisle.

It made sense to keep her and her finery out of the direct sun as much as possible, but the ceremony was now officially starting late. The minister didn't seem to share his impatience, and the man's peaceful smile was beginning to annoy him. At least the organist they'd brought in played something soothing.

Morgan watched as Minna rushed across the big kitchen to the sliders, but the relief he felt rebounded into a case of bad nerves he'd never felt before in his life. She got only close enough to the glass to wave to the minister before she made a shooing gesture to Morgan to make him turn away. The sisters had been rabid on the notion of no prewedding peeks.

The minister touched his arm to remind him to turn, then stepped into position and signaled the organist. The tune changed to something else, but not the one Morgan expected. He waited while the minister walked up the aisle to the flower-decked arbor that Lucy and her daughter had set up beyond the canopy in the sun. There'd be just enough flowery shade for the three of them to stand under while they did the speaking part of the ceremony.

Morgan waited for the minister's nod, then walked up the aisle without a notion of keeping time with anything but his impatience and now suddenly, his chagrin. People he'd known or done business with his whole life had showed up to witness this, and he heartily wished now he hadn't opened himself up for this kind of public exposure.

He'd reached the flower arbor when the tune changed again to the one he recognized. But the moment he heard those first notes, the surprise vows he'd memorized darted out of his head like swallows out of a barn.

He couldn't get them back so he was glad Selly hadn't known about them. He was too edgy to feel disappointed. He'd figure a way to let the minister know he'd changed his mind, but for now he had to concentrate on what was about to happen.

He'd seen Em and Minna earlier and thought they looked beautiful in their bright finery. One was dressed in soft pinks, the other in light yellows, though he hadn't remembered which until he saw them again now as they walked down the aisle. He'd never seen them so dressed up. They'd looked years younger than their almost sixty years, and both were almost girlish with excitement.

But the moment he saw Selena, he was blind to them, and he was suddenly unaware of anything or anyone but his bride. She was dressed from head to toe in white satin and lace, and like some fairy princess come to life, she was spangled with tiny little sparkles. When she got close enough to move into the sunlight for the space of about a yard, all those little sparkles seemed to explode into a million stars.

He took her hand as she reached him and he remembered to turn toward the minister, though he couldn't look away from her. He could see her face through the netting of her veil, and he hoped her smile was more relaxed than it looked.

The minister finally got his attention and he tried to follow the ceremony, feeling the tremor in Selena's hand as the man nattered on. He'd thought this would take little more than five minutes, but it felt like an hour. He managed to speak in all the right places, say all the right things, but the words he'd meant to add were coming back only a syllable at a time.

Then the moment arrived, and he put the wedding band on Selena's finger. This was the moment he'd privately asked the minister to give him, but now he wished he'd not given in to that rare—very rare—romantic urge.

The run of panic he felt was equally rare, but he made himself look up from the ring and he tried to see through that veil and look Selena in the eye. He suddenly remembered the words, but just as suddenly he realized they weren't fancy enough for this.

Why had he thought he'd want to say such private things in front of a crowd? His throat felt scratchy and hot, and he decided to keep them for later. Morgan gave the preacher a prompting look and after a moment, he went on.

The only thing Morgan really listened for then was for the part that finished this off. At last he heard the minister say,

"You may now kiss your bride, Mr. Conroe."

Morgan was never so glad to hear an order in his life, and he made short work of Selena's fragile veil. And then he was kissing her, realizing only when he felt the little poke Em gave him that it had gone on long enough.

The minister had barely intoned the words, "I now present Mr. and Mrs. Morgan Conroe," before Morgan was moving Selena down the aisle, so relieved to have it done that he had force himself to keep in mind how long Selly's dress was and keep his pace reasonable.

The biggest part of the crowd had left the house, and only cleanup people were still around. Peggy Hatcher had caught Selena's bouquet in the front hall two hours ago, and that had been the start of the party breaking up. Em and Minna had gone into the living room to sit down for a few minutes, glad Morgan had ordered them to relax a while.

Selly was napping upstairs, the first one in a week, and the sisters wished they'd had the sense to do the same. Particularly now, as the Swisher brothers wandered into the living room and cornered them.

''How'd you like the food, ladies?'' Sarge Swisher asked as he walked over to the wing chairs where she and Minna were seated. Dooley swaggered along behind him.

No doubt the bachelor brothers had been delighted to have Morgan hire them to handle the barbecue. Neither of the old coots passed up an opportunity to flirt with either her or Minna—and every other female under eighty—but Em gave him a reasonably gracious answer.

"You done a good job on the beef, but that one salad needed a little less vinegar."

Sarge and Dooley were tall and as lean as fence posts. Sarge almost creaked as he bent down to lean close. "Well, I reckon that salad's like Dooley and me. We could use a little more sugar in our mix. So how 'bout the four of us get out tonight and catch a show?"

Em felt her face go red, and she was embarrassed to feel a girlish thrill over yet another feckless invitation that she and Minna would normally turn down without a thought.

But maybe it was the wedding that made it harder this time, or maybe all the flowers, or the fact that Selena and Morgan were so happy. All had come right between the man and woman she and Minna had lovingly mothered. Now even better things were ahead for them all, so many things that it made Em feel downright optimistic. And a little foolhardy.

"Don't know how long this clean up'll run," she said noncommittally.

Dooley hunkered down in front of them, his knees crackling like popcorn. As usual, he had a toothpick in one corner of his mouth and he always talked around it. What got Em's attention this time was the twinkling gleam in his dark eyes.

"We was wonderin' if you girls'd mind doin' us raft of those cinnamon pecan rolls. Those ones you took over to the rental office and to Lucy's were prime."

"Like to made my eyes water with pleasure," Sarge put in. "Even better than a piece of that lemon meringue."

Dooley nodded and worked the toothpick to the other side of his mouth.

"Same for me. That meringue was good, the chocolate cream pie was good, but those rolls beat 'em all."

Dooley grinned. "Sarge and I been tryin' to figure out just what it is we gotta catch you girls at to get that kind of payoff for our silence."

Rattled, Em sent Minna a panicked look. Minna was aghast, but she was the first to think of something to say. She visibly relaxed and then smiled like an angel.

"That's quite a compliment, boys. I'm wondering if you've seen that new movie we've been wanting to see? The one about the woman who decides to take in all those little kids. Then she gets sick."

Em knew neither man would find that storyline appealing. She and Minna hadn't. But the point was to keep these cowboy Casanovas at bay, and it took a lot to discourage them.

They were all too old for this kind of nonsense, and it was a fact that neither man had ever been serious about a woman in their lives, at least not serious enough to marry. She and Minna had decided a long time ago not to fall for their invitations.

It was much better to be known as the women who'd said no than to say yes and get jilted later on like every other female in this part of Texas who'd fallen for the Swisher boys.

But the worst part of this particular invitation was the hint of blackmail. Just how much had the Swishers found out? Surely not the details, but only that the pies and rolls delivered to Lucy's and the rental office had been thank-you payoffs to the owners and employees for keeping secret the favors they'd done.

She and Minna still hadn't decided when to confess to Morgan and Selena what they'd done with the rental cars and the flowers from "C." Or if they should.

Sarge was quicker to recover from the unappealing prospect of spending his money on the show Minna described, though his voice sounded a little less flirty.

"Well, I reckon that'd be a fine one to see."

Em should have been aggravated by that too, but she couldn't account for the tickle of excitement that went through her. The Swisher brothers might be the most incorrigible bachelors in this part of Texas, but they were certainly the most entertaining.

And since she and Minna were staying in Coulter City tonight so Morgan and Selena could have their wedding night in an empty house before they set off for their honeymoon tomorrow afternoon, maybe it wouldn't be so bad to let the

Swisher brothers pay for a couple tickets to the show. And maybe a box of popcorn and some sweets.

Nobody needed to fall for anybody, and surely her reputation and Minna's wouldn't suffer for it.

Em looked over at her sister. The wordless communication between them confirmed her sudden reluctance to give the brothers the usual what-for and say no. Minna looked as flushed and excited as she was, so Em reckoned they might as well go to the show.

It was after seven before Em and Minna hugged them goodbye and left for Coulter City. Though Selena hadn't needed a nap for a few days, she was glad she'd taken a short one that afternoon to make up for the sleep she'd lost last night.

It had been such a perfect day. The photographer Morgan had hired had taken some beautiful shots of them and the sisters. Once he'd finished, they'd changed out of their formal clothes and joined their guests. Though it had been just a little over three weeks since she'd come to Conroe, if felt longer, particularly since the closer they'd got to the wedding, the less she'd seen of Morgan.

And now the luxury of being able to stay little more than arm's length away from him most of the day had given her a feeling of contentment she'd never felt before.

Selena wasn't certain she'd ever seen Morgan so relaxed and sociable, though he'd always enjoyed having guests. Em and Minna had had a ball, getting to practice their gift for hospitality without the usual chores and serving duties. She'd seen Morgan gently intervene only three times to keep them from taking on something he'd hired others to take care of.

It had been after she'd come downstairs from her nap in late afternoon that the glittering heat she'd seen in Morgan's eyes all day had shown signs of intensifying. There were still workers in the house and outside, and Em and Minna had still been around, so other than a few stolen kisses in a hall or in a temporarily empty room, that heat had little chance of being ignited.

Now they were alone in the front hall. Morgan closed the door, then turned to put his hands on her waist. He smiled down at her, the lazy curve to his mouth letting her know he relished the idea that they were finally alone in the big house.

"Glad you married me?" he asked, and Selena's smile widened.

"So far."

''I'm glad you didn't take your hair down.''

Selena gently pulled away and turned to loop her arm through his. ''I'm glad too,'' she said as his arm tightened and he started them forward. ''Should we have supper now?''

''Is that your way of saying you'd rather wait till full dark before we go upstairs?''

''Now that everyone's gone...yes, though I'm not really hungry.''

''Neither am I. How 'bout we go in the parlor and open that champagne? It ought to be chilled enough by now.''

Selena went in with him and he led her to the sofa to sit down before he opened the bottle. He didn't spill a drop, and Selena smiled at that, then waited as he poured some in the wine flutes Em and Minna had had engraved with their names and the date. He sat down and handed her the flute.

"Shall I do the honors?"

Selena nodded, and Morgan lifted his glass. "To a long, happy marriage."

They drank the toast and Morgan took both wine flutes and placed them on the tray.

"Minna put out the family Bible for us to add our names to."

He took her hand and they stood to walk over to the table that held the old, oversized leather-bound book. Morgan opened it and together they read through the list of names. Each name had been hand-printed, with signatures below. Selena noted that at one time the Conroe family had been large, until Buck's generation when he'd been an only child. Morgan had also been an only child.

"It looks like we should do something about the dwindling names," Selena said, and Morgan chuckled.

"How about an even half dozen? We've had a few twins here and there, so it might not take long. My grandfather was a fraternal twin, but his sister didn't survive her first week. I don't recall what they called it back then, but it was something that wouldn't have happened nowadays."

As he'd said that, Morgan had bent down to print his name then make his signature under it before he handed her the pen. Selena wrote her name to the right of his, adding her middle name, Elaine. Morgan's middle name was Ransom, and she could see now that Ransom had been the maiden name of one of his great-grandmothers.

Selena wasn't certain where her middle name had come from, and maybe that was why the parlor and the history it contained had always fascinated her. And now she was officially a part of that rich, ongoing history of the Conroe family.

Someday their children would be brides and grooms and they'd add their names and signatures, along with their spouses'. Selena handed Morgan the pen and he set it down before he closed the Bible.

Then he took her into his arms and she knew the moment his lips covered hers that he had no intention of waiting around until after sunset to go upstairs. And sure enough, he eased away and broke off the kiss to bend down and sweep her up into his arms.

He grinned into her flushed face. "You already guessed I'd run out of patience, didn't you?"

Selena merely smiled and tightened her arms around his neck to press close as he strode from the room. He carried her up the long staircase then on down the hall to the very end. Despite his orders to Min and Em that day, the two women had come up sometime that afternoon after Morgan had changed out of his formal clothes and showered.

Selena hadn't known what more they'd done except change the sheets and put on a new bedspread, but the moment Morgan walked in the open door, she gasped. Morgan came to a sudden halt, his blue gaze going around the room, swiftly cataloging the changes. There were flowers here and there, but also dozens of vanilla candles, from tapers to short fat ones. The very masculine room had been soundly feminized.

"What're we gonna do with that many candles after tonight?" he growled, but Selena heard the amusement in his voice. He carried her to the bed, then lowered her to her feet. He was kissing her before her toes touched the floor, and the hem of the white, short-sleeved linen dress she'd changed into earlier caught on his belt buckle on the way down.

Selena drew back a little. "I think I'm caught."

Morgan glanced down, then unhooked the hem. Selena eased back a little to smooth it into place before he lifted his hands to cradle her face and deliver a tender kiss. And then he ended it and slowly withdrew. "Before I get sidetracked…"

His low voice faded to a gravely rasp and he lightly touched her hair, searching for hairpins. He started to gently remove them and Selena's eyes drifted shut with the pleasure of the search. One by one, each skein of hair fell to her shoulders and tumbled down her back until Morgan had found every hairpin. He paused to gently kiss her again, and Selena swayed a little.

She didn't open her eyes when he ended the kiss and stepped away, but she heard the hairpins scatter on the night table. Then he stepped close once more and she felt the warm intrusion of his fingers at the top button of her bodice.

Her hands came up to his waist and she held on as she felt the first button release. Morgan bent down to place a kiss on the bit of flesh he'd uncovered, and she felt her knees go a little weaker. He opened two more buttons in the same unrushed way, and she felt a nick of disappointment when he stopped.

"There was something I left out of the ceremony this morning," he told her, the sound of his low voice sending a warm sweetness through her. It was an effort to open her eyes and mentally review her memory of that morning.

"What was that?" She couldn't think of a thing the ceremony had lacked. On the other hand, she'd been so nervous and excited that there was no way she could be certain of that.

"I told the preacher I wanted to say something to you after I put the ring on your finger. I had it all planned out, but then it went out of my head. By the time it came back, it didn't sound fancy enough to say in front of folks. Everything had gone well up to that point, and I didn't want to spoil it."

The idea that Morgan had planned to say something special to her then had decided his words weren't eloquent enough to say in public sent a little ache through her. She would have wanted to hear every word, fancy or not. Particularly since she already knew it would have been heartfelt.

"Oh, Morgan, the only thing that could have spoiled today was if you'd said you'd changed your mind about marrying me. What was it you'd planned to say?''

Morgan smiled a little. ''Come sit down and I'll tell you.'' He seated her on the edge of the mattress, then actually went down on one knee in front of her. Selena giggled at the unexpected solemnity and then tried to stifle it. Morgan gave her a playfully stern look.

''You've got me on one knee, about to lay my heart on the floor at your feet, and you're giggling?''

Selena leaned forward a little to put her hands on his wide shoulders then his jaw. She made her face go suitably serious.

''I'm sorry. It's been a big day, and I'm…a little nervous.''

Morgan gave her a crooked smile. ''Me too.''

Selena leaned forward to kiss him and the thrill of being able to just kiss him like this, knowing it was completely welcome and enjoyed, still felt as wonderful as the first time she'd done it. But she was eager to hear what he'd planned to say, so she drew back and opened her eyes.

"Please, tell me," she urged softly, then marveled at the faint flush that crept up beneath his tan. Her heart had already been light with happiness but now it seemed to explode with the certainty that she was about to hear the one thing that would make everything more wonderful still.

Selena went breathless as Morgan made a gruff-voiced start.

"Remember I told you it wasn't fancy," he warned, "though it's true. And it's been true for longer than I wanted to see."

He reached up to the hand she still had on his cheek and rubbed it against his skin, as if he was savoring the feel, before he turned his head to press a kiss into her palm. Then he looked at her again and the solemnity in his eyes gripped her.

"All I have is yours, Selena, not just a percentage," he said gently. "All I am as a man, all I'll ever be, all the good things I can give you, and all the good things it's possible for a man to feel for a woman, all of that belongs to you now."

He smiled and Selena thought he was the most handsome man in the world. "Like I said, it's been that way for a while now, though I didn't want to see it. Which leaves me with one last thing. And that's to say I love you. I reckon that means you've got my heart along with everything else."

His low words lodged deep in her, but then joy whirled up like a sparkling cyclone. Her voice was a whisper.

"'I love you, Morgan. With all I have, with all I am...'"

And then she fairly threw herself into his arms. She was kissing him wildly, joyfully, and Morgan rose up to take that last half step closer to the bed. He planted his knee on the mattress and slowly lowered her backward to lie across the new bedspread.

The love words they said to each other went on and on, gasped out or growled out. Once that first flurry of need to express what they felt burned away a little, they slowly set about showing each other without words. The cloth barriers between them began to slip away. All the other barriers had fallen anyway, and soon these were gone too.

At some point, the beautiful bedspread had been pushed aside to reveal the new ivory satin sheets beneath. Neither of them would notice until later. They'd already forgotten the candles, but then, the only glow they needed for that very special first time was the glow of love that lit their hearts and flushed their skin. A glow that soon ignited a fiery passion neither of them had dreamed existed.

Like great lovers before them, including some whose names were recorded in the book downstairs, their hearts rose high with everything they felt and everything they did, until they were no longer earthbound, and the power of what they felt carried them to the sky.

Later, much later, they drifted back and touched earth again to lie in the quiet aftermath. They dozed a little, then went back to quiet words and soft declarations, until a few lazy caresses led to a few little kisses. The lips that gave those kisses began to linger once or twice and then to roam, drawing the lovers closer and deeper, then higher again. And soon enough, they found themselves reaching together for another mind-dazzling trip to the sky.